The Green of Me

Patricia Lee Gauch

THE GREEN OF ME

G. P. Putnam's Sons

New York

Library of Congress Cataloging in Publication Data
Gauch, Patricia Lee.
The green of me.
Summary: On her way to keep an important date,
seventeen-year-old Jennifer recalls events
in her past life that have lead to this journey.
I.   Title.
PZ7.G2315Gt   [Fic]   78-6606
ISBN 0-399-20647-7

to

MARGARET FRITH
my editor and friend

THE TRAIN, THE JAMES WHITCOMB
RILEY, ONCE PART OF THE FAMOUS
C & O RAILROAD LINE, IS UNIQUE
IN THAT IT EXISTS TODAY, STILL
FULFILLING ITS DAILY SCHEDULE
ALONG THE HUNDRED-YEAR-OLD ROUTE
BETWEEN CINCINNATI, OHIO,
AND CHARLOTTESVILLE, VIRGINIA.

Part One

THERE IS SOMETHING about a train I like. So
much better than a jet. I'm not sure exactly what.
Maybe it's the attendant saying, here let me help you with
that bag. Maybe the metal windowsills I can set my Coke
on, or the wide, soft seats I can curl up in. Or the way the
hills and towns and factories fly by as if they're some kind
of travel movie. You can feel the cogs and wheels clicking
under you. Hear the whistle.

Yes, maybe that's it. You can feel a train, hear it. A
friendly monster. Friendly, but no-nonsense. In a hurry, a
schedule to meet, someplace to go, 340 miles to Charlottesville, Virginia, ticking off the miles. Maybe it will
get there late, but it will get there. My father would say
it's something dependable. I guess I need to know that.

And this time I'm going with it. Jennifer Lynn Cooper
on her way. Ticking off the miles. A schedule to meet. I
rode a train once before from Cincinnati to Louisville
with my grandmother. Felt it. Saw the telephone poles
streak by. I had to sit on her lap the whole way, along
with a basket of egg-salad sandwiches. Not today. Look at
me, even a seat just like anyone else. The same as that
businessman with the wide lapels across the aisle, the

same as that gray-haired woman with the white sneakers (white sneakers!), the soldier sleeping with his feet up on the seat in front of him. There's another difference; I can't even remember where Grandma and I were going. This time I know where I'm going. Well, partly. Maybe not what I'm going to say or do. But I know where I have to go to figure it out.

I wonder if all of them know. Seat 20, Seat 21, Seat 22, Seat 23. We watch each other, share the dining room, the water cooler, the john, but don't know anything more. Who we are, where we're going, if it matters to someone waiting on the other end.

There are things I could tell them about me. An entrance form, maybe, for nonsmoker, Car 30. Name: Jennifer Lynn, etc., age, 17, parents, yes, James and Dorothy (Jim and Dot to friends). No brothers or sisters (cousins enough, Rosemary, Rob, Letty). Address: Waterbury, Ohio, Cape Cod house on leafy street, two arm's lengths away from neighbors' Cape Cod house on leafy street. Same size, same shape. Education: high school and ———.

Extracurricular activities: reading, piano, swimming. No, there's more: dancing alone on the beach at night, arguing ideas with anyone who will argue, eating raspberries and raspberries . . . and raspberries, sitting in yoga lotus position over Beethoven or the Beatles, thinking.

Reason for riding this train: ah, back at the beginning. Reason? To keep a date. God, that sounds simple. Almost like an appointment. There is the orthodontist's and the doctor's and the haircutter's. And this one. No, not the same. Those you make two weeks in advance, and you don't think about them. This one? I made the train reservation thirty days ago, March 31, the day after I got the letter, but the date? I believe everything you've ever been or done makes what you are and what you do now. I believe that. So maybe I made this date ten years ago, maybe more, when life seemed to stand still, when I used to lie in bed and squeeze my eyes together and see all the stars and the moons and the grayness that hadn't any shape spinning around me. Things moved, but not me. So sure. Sure that my mother would always be there when the bee stung me in the violet patch, that my father would always say, "Climb in bed, Jennifer Lynn, and tell me a story," that my grandmother would always have the hot oatmeal cereal and the cow creamer set on the table before I even got up, that a best friend would always be there calling me by a string and tin can between our houses.

So sure. All of it. Dependable. Like this train. And me at the center.

Maybe that's when I made the date. Or maybe a little later when I first felt the rhythm, slow, like a train pulling out of a station. When I began to suspect that the red helium balloon I left floating on my ceiling the night before might be only a wrinkled piece of rubber, lying on my bedroom floor in the morning. That "alone" might be a real word. That darkness was very dark. That I was the center of a very small universe indeed, and that the world might be moving, and so maybe was I.

Maybe that was when I made the date.

"HERE'S THE BIG KINDERGARTNER! All right, Jennifer Lynn, crawl in bed with me. Now . . . tell me the one about the sheep. That's the one I like best."

"Not sheep, Daddy. Goats. 'The Three Billy Goats Gruff.'"

"Yes, that's it. Go ahead."

"Really?"

"Really."

"Once upon a time there were three Billy Goats Gruff . . ."

"Who said baa, baa, baa."

"Daddy! I said they were *goats*."

"Oh, yes, goats! I've got it now. Go ahead."

"And they all decided the grass was longer and sweeter on the other side of the bridge."

"What bridge? The Brooklyn Bridge?"

"No, Daddy. The troll's bridge!"

"Troll! I don't like scary stories. Is this a scary story, Jennifer Lynn?"

"No!"

"Are you sure?"

"Daddy!"

"All right, all right, go on . . . but not too scary."

"Well, the baby Billy Goat Gruff started across the bridge. Clip, clop, clip, clop."

"What's that?"

"His feet!"

"Sorry, it was scary."

". . . and a voice from beneath the bridge said, "WHO'S THAT CLIP-CLOPPING OVER MY BRIDGE!"

"Your voice has certainly gotten gruff."

"That's the troll!"

"I thought you said the baby billy goat was gruff."

"He is!"

"Well, how can the troll be gruff, too?"

"It's the billy goat's *name*, Daddy!"

"Maybe they're brothers."

"Daddy!"

"Or cousins."

"Daddy!"

"You'd better tell the story about the three pigs instead. They don't have any troll relatives."

"Oh, Daddy . . ."

J ENNIFER NESTLED into the sealskin coat as the car purred along. She never really minded going for long impossible rides with Grandma Stokes. Everything inside the car was shiny, even though it had to be twenty years old. The ashtrays, the door handles, the strips all mirrored Jenny's face in their stretchy or squat way. From her cozy perch against her grandma's arm, Jenny wrinkled her nose at the ashtray; it wrinkled back — a squat monster. Jennifer stuck out her tongue. The monster did, too. Satisfied with its accuracy, Jennifer snuggled back into the silky softness.

She didn't even mind that Grandma was bringing Rosemary back to spend the night, too. For a cousin and a two-year-older one, Rosemary wasn't too bad sometimes. She was leaning over the seat, her chin by Grandma's shoulder. The trouble with having a ten-year-old around, of course, was that she thought she owned the world. And Grandma.

"And can I have the cot next to your bed tonight, Grandma," she was asking. Rosemary had blond ringlets all over her head, and blue blue eyes so bright that people — sometimes strangers — stopped and said, "What a pretty child."

Even now on a lazy Saturday when Jennifer had just managed to find some clean blue jeans and a three-time worn print shirt, Rosemary had on a starched white blouse and plaid slacks, and her eyes seemed wide and bright just talking to Grandma.

Jennifer blinked at her reflection in the ashtray, trying to look bright and wide-eyed. It looked like the monster had a tic.

"Of course, of course, the bed by Grandma." Grandma was smiling. Her hair was dark, not a strand of gray, even though she was over seventy years old, and her skin was pink and smooth, stretched over broad cheekbones and a sturdy, strong chin. This was a soft grandma, but an eminently strong grandma, a grandma who knew how to nail the cupboard door back on with two hefty thunks. A grandma who knew how to unplug the toilet. Who could fix the electric plug that came apart in Jenny's hand when she tugged too hard. But a grandma who always had her hand ready to form a partnership with Jenny in a crowded grocery store, or in the dark when Jenny got to sleep next to her.

Jenny didn't like that Rosemary would be next to Grandma, but she didn't say it. After all, Jenny got to be with Grandma lots, every time there was a holiday and mother was working. Rosemary hardly ever came to stay all night. One cot away would be all right.

At 9201 Abbeville Road, Grandma pulled in the tiny, antique car, neatly and carefully, and the girls hopped out, running ahead to wait at the door. The icy cold pricked Jennifer's legs and she hopped miserably from one foot to the other. Rosemary picked up a ball of snow and, with a secret glint put it behind her back and danced up to Jennifer.

"Jennifer," she smiled, "you trust people too much." And she took the ball of snow and squished it on Jennifer's head. Now Jennifer's straggly brown hair looked miserably frosted, but she just reached up and picked the snow out, staring down at her shoes as she did.

She hated Rosemary. Truly she did. At least at that moment she did. Rosemary was sinewy-strong. Her fingernails hurt when she squeezed Jennifer's arm, and Jennifer could never peel them off, as hard as she tried.

She didn't even say anything to Grandma when she frowned at her. "Jenny, Jenny, what have you gotten into now." She chucked Jennifer under the chin and smiled. "You have trouble staying neat!"

Jennifer twisted her mouth. No, that wasn't so, not this time. But she didn't say it out loud. Rosemary was looking at her. And it didn't matter. Inside Grandma's house Rosemary would want the ceramic animals to play with like she always did. Jennifer would pretend to want them, too, but it was a lie. Jennifer smiled to herself. What Jennifer really wanted was the dressing table and what was in it.

Maybe it didn't look so special. It was dark brown and sat rather high on spindly legs, but it had a magnificent three-split mirror in which you could see yourself three times in three different ways. If you sat just right, you could even see the back of yourself in the long mirror on the door.

Sometimes Jennifer would take out all Grandma's creams and her lipsticks and put them on just the way she wanted. Grandma never minded. She only said, "What a beautiful Jenny I have now — " But Jennifer never stopped to say thank you because when you prepared for a ball, you couldn't stop, not to say a word. If the prince were going to pick you as the most beautiful girl in the country, the dabs on your cheek had to be just so.

And your eyelashes had to be curled in a sweep. And your hair had to be brushed a hundred times (one, two, three) until the strands looked like silk (four, five) and felt like liquid (six, seven), and you had to hold your head just so (eight, nine, ten), because the way you held your head told people you were important (eleven, twelve, thirteen, fourteen). And pretty.

And when her face was creamy and pink and pretty, then she woud take out the handkerchief box and choose the one that would match her gown. Probably the lace one that hung together like airy spider webs, the one that fit in her fingers just so.

And lastly, she would open the drawer and take out the jewels. The world famous queen's jewels. She would by-pass the necklace of diamonds; they were too fat. And the three-strand pearls were long, far too long for a Princess Jenny. And the bracelets fell off her wrists, so they wouldn't do. But in the back, in the brown box that snapped, Jenny kept Grandma's ring. It was a garnet which Grandma said had been given her on her sixteenth birthday. Only Jenny knew about the ring and how Grandma had gotten it from her Uncle Hal. It was tiny, set in gold, and it didn't fit Jenny's ring finger, not yet, but it fit Jenny's middle finger just right.

The prince would notice the ring the minute they began to dance. Tiny and red and gold, and Jenny's.

The heavy door swung open and Grandma bustled in

with her packages, the two girls running ahead to stake out their territories.

"I get the green chair for the whole day," Rosemary said, squatting in the thick armchair by the fireplace.

"I'll take the spindle-back one," Jenny said. She wasn't sure why she needed it, but suddenly she could see she'd better take what she could.

"And I get the scissors first," Rosemary called out, running now to the desk and reaching into the bottom drawer.

Jenny called back, "And I get the puzzle!" That was Grandma's letter puzzle, which Jenny never had figured out but which was always an important stake.

"Oh, and I get the animals." Rosemary ran into the kitchen where Grandma kept the tiny porcelain cows and sheep and pigs on a corner shelf. "Oh, the pigs are wonderful," she shouted so Jennifer could hear. "And the lambs. I'm going to set up a whole kingdom!"

Jennifer fingered the puzzle in her hand and shrugged a secret smile as she watched Rosemary take the animals one by one into the living room, whistling. When she was sure Rosemary was busy, Jennifer meandered toward the bedroom, backward, keeping a careful eye on Rosemary playing on the floor in the living room.

She backed into the doorway and over to the dressing table. It even smelled good. Like Grandma's powder. And Jergen's hand lotion. She smiled as she crawled up on the highish bench and squeezed her arms into her sides excitedly trying to decide where to start. As she glanced up, the princess was already looking at her.

"Foolish lady," she said, "you have waited too long to get dressed. Now you must hurry!" She pursed her lips and pouted prettily at the three princesses pouting back at her. It had already started to happen. Already she wasn't Jenny.

She opened the drawer and poked at the treasure of jars and bottles in front of her. Cupping two in her hand, she unscrewed one top, smelled, then unscrewed another. They really were delicious. And all hers. Foolish Rosemary with her porcelain cows. Jennifer dabbed on a creamy base, stretching her mouth down to make her cheeks smooth, then rubbed it in. Oh, the smells. Like sugary perfume or flowers in the garden, some things wonderful.

Then the rouge. The pinkish one to match a yellow gown. Quick dabs, and a smile at the three princesses. Then the blues for the eyelids . . . or should she use green? They were hardly touched since Grandma didn't use them often. Samples, probably. There was something wonderfully fresh about using new makeup. Now she could look bright and wide-eyed. Her eyes could dance. She smiled. The three princesses smiled winningly.

She was alone in this place, wonderfully alone. And it was hers. Quickly, then, she went through the rest of the jars. The powder, the lightener, the eyelash curler, the eyelash goo. Then she brushed (one, two, three). She felt herself getting excited just thinking of the other drawer, the handkerchief and the box. But she was nearly ready.

Finally, with her hair silky and brushed and the jars and bottles closed, she looked again at her fair self and in the rear mirror at the princess behind. Then she reached, tasting each moment, for the box at the back of the drawer. It was velvety in her palm, and she pressed it against her cheek and rubbed it over her chin.

She had bent over to see it open when she heard the door

behind her. She pinched the box into her palm and looked into the mirror to see Rosemary staring at her then begin laughing.

"Oh, you clown! You silly clown. You're all smeared up. Sloppy old Jenny, can't even put her lipstick on straight." She took Jenny's arms to pull her around and saw Jenny's clasped hand.

"What do you have, Jenny?" Rosemary's eyes grew suspicious. "Are you hiding something from me?" Jenny smiled and shook her head. No words would come, but she opened the drawer a small crack and tried to squeeze the box back inside.

Rosemary's quick fingers nipped it out. "You do have something, Jenny. You silly clown." And she sat down next to her and opened the box. The velvety, cheek-soft box with the garnet ring.

"Oh, Jenny," Rosemary oohed, "it is beautiful. It is the most beautiful ring . . ." She took it out and put it on her ring finger. "And it fits me. Look, Jenny, how it fits me."

"It fits me, too," Jenny got out in a whisper, trying to retrieve it.

"But it couldn't fit your *ring* finger, it couldn't! And it just fits mine." She was holding it up to the three mirrors when Grandma came in with dust cloths over her arm, humming one of her no-songs. She stopped and took Rosemary's hand.

"Now, you've found it." She was grinning; it was pretended anger. "My sixteenth-birthday ring. My Uncle Hal gave that to me. He worked in the biggest jewelry store in town. A pure garnet, that's what it is. It looks pretty with your white skin, Rosemary," Grandma said. She looked warmly delighted to see the ring on Rosemary's finger.

"Oh, Grandma, might I have it? I would take especially good care. Truly, I would. I never lose things. Never. I still have the yellow canary from last year's carnival. Please." Her eyes begged.

Grandma sat down. "Well . . . I never thought about giving it away." (*Oh, please, Grandma, don't!*) "Of course, I can't wear it. I'm too old and fat," she chuckled warmly, smoothing down the ruffles on her tremendous bust. "And you are ten years old. That is pretty grown-up."

"Please!" Rosemary begged one more long whine.

Grandma smiled and put her arms around Rosemary and Jennifer and looked at the two girls in the center mirror. "My pretty little girls. And one wants my garnet ring. I guess I would be pretty selfish if I said no, don't you, Jenny?"

Rosemary sucked in a thrilled gasp and looked at the ring. "Then may I have it?"

"Yes, yes, Rosemary. Honestly, you children. I won't have anything left in the house at the rate I give my things to you."

But Jennifer wasn't listening. Suddenly her eyelashes felt gummy and her cheeks pasty, and she licked her lips, avoiding the three-part mirror.

JENNIFER PULLED HER TOES up into her striped flannel nightgown and folded herself into a ball under the covers. Dissatisfied with a draft that stubbornly sneaked under the covers to chill her back, she pulled the covers into an arc over her head again and included them in her ball. She had made up her mind. Tonight she was not going to go. It didn't matter that her door was shut and there was no night light on. She was nine years old, and there was no reason to crawl in bed with her mother and father. Not anymore. Not when a person was nine years old.

It would be just plain silly. She hadn't even brought Willie, her stuffed panda, into bed with her tonight. And she wasn't going to spend a lot of silly time wishing for a brother or sister to sleep in the room with her. Silly dreams, how a Jonathan or Carol could sleep in bed next to her and talk and laugh. Silly stuff. Nighttime is nighttime, with someone in the room with you or not.

Jennifer settled warmly in her ball. Anyhow, she knew all the sounds. Just night sounds. Nothing to be afraid of. That scratchy sound was the elm tree, scraping against the window as the fall wind blew through it. That clicking, Maily, the cat, taking her nighttime walk across the bureau, knocking over perfume bottles, spring lilac probably. The tinny tick-ticking, the French clock underneath her bedroom, hurrying to ten o'clock when the gongs would begin. Such loud, hollow gongs. If they only stopped for one night, maybe she could climb into her high three-quarter bed with the spools, put her head on her pillow, and go right off to sleep.

Then she wouldn't even hear night sounds.

Jennifer pulled the covers down for a moment and listened. Her parents were still whispering. Always before, that was what she waited for, waited and waited, for the whispering to stop. Then she knew she could creep in and quietly climb in on her mother's side. Before, long ago, her daddy used to call her into bed with them. There the three of them would be, trying to top each other's stories, laughing at each other, teasing. But that was long ago, when she was seven . . . or six. More and more she had to sneak in, and always after the whispering stopped.

But not tonight. Jennifer wasn't going to go. She felt that cold draft again, rushing to a place near her ear, and she rolled herself back into a ball, but this time, as she did, something creaked. *Something in the room creaked.* Jenny lay, not moving. That creaking had to be, had to be . . . the chair. She had put all of her clothes on that chair for a whole week. Her brown plaid skirt. The white blouse with the initial "J" on the pocket. At least four pairs of stockings, one stinky pair she'd had to wear twice. It was the chair, weighed down and creaking. That was it.

But she heard the sound again. A creaking. Her neck felt warm and her mouth, dry. She listened harder. What did it sound like? Maily playing in her shoes? He did that sometimes. No, no, Maily had settled into the back of her knees. She could feel him. Then, then it had to be the pipes creaking with warm water. Aunt Margaret said that sometimes happened in the night when the water just sat. But Daddy had turned off the hot water; Jennifer had seen him. "Got to save money somehow," he had said.

Jenny felt something tighten in her, something under the striped nightgown, deep in her. Then, if it wasn't the cat or the pipes or the chair, what was it?

Suddenly she knew. Someone else was in the room. She realized she shouldn't move. Not a muscle. It was important not to. Or breathe. Perhaps whoever it was wouldn't notice her there in the bed. She was small. Perhaps he would notice the box on the bureau instead; there was a pearl necklace there. He would take the pearl necklace and go away. Oh, no. It wasn't on the bureau! Stupid Jenny. She had left the box and the pearl necklace in the bathroom when she brushed her teeth. Then he might be looking around the room now for other things . . . or her. There was no creaking, but there wouldn't be, not if he were only looking. From the chair heaped with clothing, to the empty bureau with the tipped-over perfume, to her stuffed animals heaped in the corner where she had dumped them. Jenny suddenly wished she had Willie the panda with her; it helped to put her arms around his warm, stuffed self. Now she was alone.

Her lungs were full to bursting and, knowing she had to breathe and knowing she couldn't, she let the air seep out slowly. See, she could do it without it showing from the outside. Her nightgown didn't even move. Slowly, slowly she let the air out. He wouldn't see the blankets move. He wouldn't see her. He wouldn't. But somehow she knew — he did see her.

Stiff in her ball, and now growing cold, she listened for his footsteps, waited for him. Then all at once her face softened. He was still there, she knew it, but, more important, there were no voices from the other room. Her mother and father must have dropped off to sleep. She could go then. She hadn't wanted to, but now she *had* to.

She caught herself. But he was still there, standing somewhere in the room, waiting. She would have to move quickly. She would throw off the covers . . . no, no, first she would have to pull up her nightgown so she wouldn't trip. It would be awful to trip in front of him. He would get her for certain. First, she'd pull up the nightgown, then she'd push the covers back and simply make a dash for the door. If he were in front of it, well, she'd tear him away with her fingers. He loomed so black and huge, like a shadow that had a sideways, but she had to go or he'd only get closer. And without the bear or a brother or sister or heat or light, she couldn't *not* go.

There was the pause first. The get-ready pause. There was her head telling her body to act right, not to stumble or fall, not to miss the doorknob, not to let the door catch on the rug and fail to open, but to move that fast past the door, across the hall, to open the other door. That fast. No mistakes.

Slowly, she uncurled her toes. And legs. And slowly she inched the nightgown up around her thighs. And slowly she moved her fingers to the edge of the blanket, took a deep, pinching breath and . . . flung the blankets back into the dark, sprang from the bed, seized the doorknob, pulled it open, tears squeezing at her eyes, and finally pulled open the door across the hall . . . softly now, then waited inside the door of her parents' room.

She had made it. He hadn't followed her or stopped her or stood in her way. She pushed her wrist across her mouth, hiding a smile, as if she had fooled someone. Got away with it. She *had* gotten away with it, and she wasn't alone. And she wouldn't be alone any longer, not tonight. And she would sleep. She looked into the darkened, shade-drawn room. It was terribly dark, but she would squeeze in on her mother's side, and her mother would turn and gather her close to her under the covers and keep her warm. And Jenny would sleep. Finally.

Jenny moved toward the mounds, and that the mounds were moving didn't register, at first. She was simply so relieved. But her thigh caught the edge of the bed and tumbled off some papers, and a head poked up angrily.

"Jenny, you?" Jenny felt her heart beating in her throat. She knew this shadow. It was Daddy and he was mad.

"Mama?" she heard herself say. "I was just coming to sleep with . . ." But even as her father moved toward her, she saw her mother wordlessly pull up the covers and watch. Just watch.

"This is the last time . . ." her father was saying through teeth tightened in a terrible anger. "Never come into this room" — he was squeezing her arm and pushing her into the hallway — "at night again. You sleep" — and Jenny could see his eyes black in the moonlight shining in the

hall window — "in your *own* room" — and he was holding her tight against the wall — "*with your door shut.*"

And to her at that moment clearly he hated her. It sat
in her like a shadow you could see sideways. And when he
let go of her nightgown, he dropped his hands and turned
his back, and she stared at the closed door and turned
around and opened the door into her own room with the
high three-quarter bed and the oak branches easing themselves against the windows in response to the wind, and
she shut the door.

"NO ONE IS GOING TO COME, Nancy. I just
know it! No one is going to come."

"Maybe ten cents a cup for lemonade is too much."

"Maybe. I mean, everybody's gone. The Armstrongs left
for Canada."

"The Coxes and the Joneses went to Howell Lake."

"And where are the cars!"

"It's awful."

"I know. It's awful."

(pause)

"It's not really so awful."

"Hmmmm?"

"I love sitting under this willow tree, even though it's

not by the water. Even though its arms are crooked and its knees knobby."

"It seems like it should have toads and frogs living around it, doesn't it?"

"Oh, yes, in little weedy houses with plates on the tables . . ."

"And peanut butter and jam in the pots."

"And rabbits come to visit in jackets with watches in their pockets . . ."

"And foxes and badgers just waiting behind the pine trees to burst in upon everyone for tea!"

"Oh, no! Look what we've done to our willow tree!"

"It's crowded! It's crowded!"

(pause)

"Nancy, did you have willow trees in California?"

"No, we had palm trees, though."

"Oh."

"But I like willow trees better."

"Do you, do you really?"

"Hmmmmm."

(pause)

"When the Jenkins moved out, I never thought someone ten years old would move in. I never did."

"The last time I moved, there was no one my age on the whole block."

"And you're an only child . . . do people call you that, too, Nancy? Only child?"

"Yup."

"I don't like it much."

"Me either. My mother says it sounds like it's a disease. Or a virus."

(pause)

"Do you mind being one?"

"What?"

"An only child?"

"Sometimes."

"On Sundays when everybody goes off to visit somebody?"

"Yes! And on vacations when you have to play alone in a place you've never been before."

"Swing alone!"

"Build sand palaces alone!"

"And when everyone goes in for the night and you have to walk home alone under the street lights."

"And the shadows won't let you be!"

"And at night when everyone else is in bed and you're still awake in your own room."

"Yes, and the door's closed."

(pause)

"You know, Nancy, I am really glad you moved next door."

"I'm glad my bedroom window looks into yours!"

"Me, too!"

(pause)

"Want one more cup of lemonade, while we wait?"

"Just one more."

JENNIFER SPLASHED the cold water up on her face. Well water might be delicious to taste, or that's what her mother said, but it was a horrible way to wake up in the morning. At a cottage you have to expect things like that, her mother always said. Jennifer shuddered. How could anyone ever really expect water so cold it made your skin prickle in goose bumps.

She turned and handed the towel to her friend, Nancy, standing barefoot in the doorway. Not wholly awake at all, she took it and put it over her shoulder, then sleepily dipped her two hands into the sink.

Neither of them was talking. Jennifer's father had had to drive in last night after work all the way from the city, and even Nancy had learned the best thing to do in the morning was wait. See what kind of mood he was in. See how tired he was. Just wait.

Jennifer edged the door open to smell the bacon sizzling and shrinking in the frying pan, the old blackened pan Mother had bought at that noisy, shouting country auction. It was the best smell to wake up to, particularly at the cottage where the wooden walls had their own sweet smell.

Nancy shuddered and wiped her face dry, leaving it covered with the towel for a minute. It probably helped somehow. Then sleepily she tiptoed behind Jennifer into the fireplace room, the only permanent name one could give the main room in the cottage. At breakfast it was the eating room. On a rainy day it was the card room. At night, when the wind came up and everyone pulled their chairs around the fire, it was the sitting room. It could only be the fireplace room. That was general enough.

Jennifer's mother turned around and held her fingers to her lips, "Shhhhh," she said. Jennifer nodded. She knew. She knew. Nancy nodded. She knew, too.

Jennifer tiptoed with exaggeration over to the stove with her plate, pushing aside the bowl of hard-boiled eggs her mother put out every day for snacking. Right now she wanted a fried one sunny-side up to dip her bacon in. Nancy nudged in beside her, watching the frying pan spatter with the four eggs nuzzling in beside the already cooked bacon.

Jennifer closed her eyes and took in a long, sweet smell of it. Hmmmm. Even her toes didn't seem so cold.

Her mother was gently prying the curled, crispy edges up when a voice boomed from the bedroom.

"BRRRRRRRRRR!" It shook itself out like a bear's fur full of water.

Jennifer sat back, not quite sure what to expect from around the corner.

"Morning! Morning!" The voice was still not directed anywhere exactly, so no one answered. Carefully.

Then it came around the corner, its eyelids wrinkled and puffy with sleep, mere slits to reveal dark eyes. The little bit of hair it had was frizzled, standing almost on end, and it was holding a geometric-pattern Indian blanket around it, underneath which poked two spindly legs.

"Bacon!" her father yawned. Still everyone was cautious.

Then suddenly he crouched, squinting his eyes in a wizened way, wrinkling his nose and twisting his hands together, as if he were washing them.

"Long ago . . ." he said in a voice, creaking with age, "when I used to hunt in the wilderness of the Adirondacks . . ."

Jennifer began to feel better. Her father had never been to the Adirondacks. "We used to have mighty breakfasts. Mighty!" he repeated into Nancy's wondering face.

Then he spun sharply. "And do you know *how* we cracked our eggs for breakfasts?" He crept over to the egg bowl, still crouched, taking three of the snacking eggs into his hands.

Mother looked as if she might say something, but his grandiose speech was gusting like a summer wind, not to be stopped. "Did I crack them on the side of the dish? No. That wasn't for a wilderness man!" He turned to Jennifer. "With a knife perhaps? *Never.* That was sissy stuff. We cracked our eggs . . . like this . . ."

And he threw the three eggs, up, up to the top of the pitched ceiling where they cracked in a mass of wet, flying yolk and white, a rain of it, landing in splots on the table, on the chairs, on the fireside hearth, on his forehead and Nancy's arms. All over.

Mother just stood, swallowing a laugh between pressed lips. Jennifer grabbed her mouth with her hand and started to tear from holding the laugh in so tightly. Nancy closed her eyes and sniggered. Everyone was looking at the egg-spattered potentate. Waiting.

Then, sheepishly, almost embarrassedly, he hunched his shoulders and started to snigger, an inside snigger, that spread into an apologetic grin which worked like an unhooked latch on the others, and Mother started to laugh out loud, sitting down on the rocker, shaking her head from side to side at the eggy mess. Nancy started to laugh out loud, laugh, until tears edged down her cheeks. And Jennifer laughed, too. It was all right.

"Next time," he said, crossing his legs with that same embarrassment, "would someone warn me when they put raw eggs in the snacking bowl?"

But no one promised a thing.

"AM I EVER GLAD you're home, Jenny!"

"Nanc, hey. Let me grab some cherries. What's up?"

"Let's go outside by the willow."

"What is it?"

"Well . . ."

"Yes?"

"We're moving."

"Not now, not when you're in sixth grade!"

"Yes. In two months."

(pause)

"Two months?"

"Back to California."

"So far?"

"My father is getting a really super job at a new company. I'm going to have a new bedroom set with an extra twin bed."

"Oh, that's . . . that's really nice, Nanc. You sound happy."

"I am — two twin beds! You'll be able to sleep in your own bed when you come to visit."

"That sounds great . . . I'll like that a lot."

"You sound funny."

"No, I'm just surprised, that's all. Who will I play Monopoly with?"

"Silly, we haven't played Monopoly in a year."

"Tick-tack-toe."

"Jenny!"

"No, I'm kidding. Just kidding. If you promise to give me St. Charles Place and a twin bed, I'll coax my mom into letting me come to California."

"Will you, Jenny?"

"Sure. . . . Nancy?"

"Yes?"

"California is a long way from Ohio, isn't it?"

J ENNIFER SAT with her back against the door, waiting. The windowpanes had been etched mightily by Jack Frost during the night, and the snow peeped up over the bottom of the window frame in soft mounds. Ordinarily, Jenny would have worried about her legs freezing when she ran to catch the school bus. But not today. It was Christmas, and if it hadn't been cold and icy and snowy, she would have been disappointed.

The problem at the moment was waiting for the clock to strike its seven o'clock bells. Only then could she go downstairs. But it couldn't be long. Jenny rolled her eyes into closed eyelids, trying to imagine the tree and the gifts under it. She supposed it was silly caring, now that she was twelve, but she did. Maybe there would be the sled she had asked for. Or that silly stuffed mole with the brown button eyes. Maybe her mother had remembered she wanted the heather-blue cashmere sweater.

The slow dongs of the clock startled Jenny even though she had been waiting for them.

She gathered up her long nightgown and started out her door, shouting as she went, "Hey, Mom. Dad. It's seven o'clock." She guessed that in a lot of houses packs of kids were screaming down the stairs, but, being alone, her mother and father were the only sharers. And it was the one time when it was all right to be alone, to have that magic moment all to yourself.

"Damn it. I don't like it." Jenny heard her father's voice grumble from his bedroom. She smiled. Her father wasn't too swift in the morning, particularly Christmas morning. She was thinking about that when she reached the fourth stair and her mother grabbed her arm. "You can't go down. Not yet. I have to get something ready. Wait. Wait," she bubbled.

Jenny's mother bounced down the stairs like a teenager. She loved Christmas and her feeling about it spread all over Jenny. Jenny watched her mother's robe trail behind her as she turned the corner. The corridor of space she had passed through still bubbled. Her mother was something, all right; even Jenny knew that.

She was invincible, all freckly and wide-eyed, and plump as a spring robin, but bent on her ways, particularly when it came to Jenny. Stepping in her mother's way was a little bit like stepping in front of a Mack truck with a smile painted on its face . . . well, a pickup truck maybe.

Jenny sat on the stair and shook her head. It was impossible to refuse.

"Almost ready. Almost ready," her mother chirped from the next room. "Wait a minute. All right, all right." It was a steady stream of patter, which Jenny didn't even try to interrupt.

"Come down now," she called.

Jenny stepped down, grinning, trying to imagine. Since her mother had started working again, events were sometimes delayed; probably she had to finish wrapping a present. Or maybe, it was a present too large for under the Christmas tree. Jenny nodded to herself. That was probably it.

"Now," her mother directed, "close your eyes and walk straight ahead."

Jenny took deep smells of the Christmas around her. The balsam pine with its sweet tinges of Canadian woods. Some kind of metallic wrapping paper smell. The dish of walnuts her mother had put out the night before with the nut cracker. Oh, it was delicious. But then she suddenly smelled a new smell. And heard an unmotherlike rustle.

"Now, Mom?" she called.

Her mother was right in front of her. "Now," she said.

Jenny opened her eyes and looked straight ahead. But it was too wonderful! Sitting in her mother's arms was a white and black, scraggly-haired puppy with one black ear at a curious tilt.

Jenny simply couldn't believe what she saw.

"Is it mine?" she said tentatively. It wasn't that she didn't get gifts, she did, but she had always wanted a dog, a dog to run with, to be home when she got there, to sleep with, to touch, to love. All those things. So when her mother nodded, she grabbed him rather too roughly from her mother's arms.

"Oh, puppy, you're scraggly just like me, and I love you." The puppy squealed at the change of hands, and when Jenny put him down, his back legs crossed and he tipped over on his rear. "You even walk like me," Jenny whispered to him, scratching his tipped ear. He licked her salty fingertips.

"What about your other gifts, Jen," her mother said, and Jenny smiled and walked over toward the tree. The puppy propped himself up and walked after her.

"Oh, no! Look, Mom, he followed me!"

To test the experiment, Jenny walked back toward the dining room. The puppy scooted and toppled and hopped after her. Jenny quickly sidled around the corner. The puppy, bewildered, lowered his rear, then in an uneasy lurch careened around the corner like an unmanned tricycle. He had found her.

"Oh, you are very silly," Jenny said and she sat down. "Will you follow me anywhere?" The puppy licked her fingertips again, this time tucking her little finger into his mouth for a chew. "You would, wouldn't you? You're a tagalong. That's what you are."

"Sounds like a name to me." Her mother smiled, the delight at her gift spreading up into the freckles all over her face.

"Tag. Oh, yes, Tag." Jenny pressed his wiggling body against her face and tipped her neck back as he licked her again. "You really are wonderful." She felt so whole, sitting there in a heap in the dining room, with the tiny, wriggling, warm thing licking and nibbling and loving her. So whole.

She didn't even notice her father at first. When she looked up, there was a deep frown on his face, his brow deeply cut in concern. Jenny felt that tightness somewhere in her stomach, but she turned away. It was probably Christmas. Daddy hated Christmas. Really hated it. He could be silly and funny and warm. Sometimes. But on Christmas, not very often.

"This is quite impossible," he said, loud enough, to Jenny's mother.

"Please, Jim." Jennifer's mother's look pleaded.

"All right, let's be sensible, Jenny. Your mother is never sensible. How can we have a dog? I work until seven. Your mother works until five. You don't get home until four. It is impossible. Who will take care of the dog? Who will train it? Who will feed it?"

Jenny didn't know what he was saying. She suddenly held the puppy closer.

Her father must have read her bewilderment.

"I am saying we have to take the dog back to the animal shelter. It would not be fair to the dog to keep him. It would not be fair to us. It is impossible."

"Don't be silly, Jim." Jenny's mother grinned at him, trying to tease away his seriousness. "Of course, we can do it."

"Damn it." He was starting to glower darkly. "I say we can not. Why do you put me in this position? It is wrong. Dead wrong! Wrong!"

Jenny was beginning to understand, darkly. He was saying she couldn't have the puppy.

"But, Jim, you agreed last night . . ."

"I never really agreed. I paused, and you took up the cause in my hesitation. I never *really* agreed. Do you hear me!"

It was getting terribly loud. Again. Jenny put her hands over her ears and squeezed her eyes. The puppy discovered a ribbon on her nightgown and started to pull it irreverently. Even his tiny paws scrambling for balance on her lap suddenly pained Jenny.

"I'm sorry, Jenny. I could have waited until tomorrow to tell you," her father was saying, "but it would only be that much harder. You can play with the puppy today, but he goes back tomorrow. That is final."

Jenny didn't answer. She took her finger and ran it down the scraggly coat of the puppy. In the living room the French clock donged its tinny half hour.

IT WAS A HAZY SUMMER DAY, the sort where the heat seemed to hang blue over the clear amber lake like a translucent cloud. A faint hum of flies, springing from one object to another, droned their own annoying music. Jennifer followed her father down to the marshy shoreline, watching his thin, wiry stride, and listening.

"It's only a half mile or so, Jennifer, just a nice healthy swim."

Jennifer nodded, even though her father didn't turn to see. She supposed he knew she was nodding.

"The thing to do is take long, restful strokes."

Jennifer nodded. Even though she had swum parts of the distance between the shore and the island, the boat had always been rowed alongside. Clearly, this was a little crazy for a Jennifer to be doing. But this summer had been that way. Joey, the boy next door, asking her to go two lakes over, just to catch a soft-backed turtle. That village girl asking her to come to her house, a completely strange house with farm smells that Jenny didn't recognize and runny-nosed children with all-alike faces. Now Dad asking her to swim the lake with him since Joey had had to go to the city. Didn't Dad know by now she would rather watch. Or would she? She used to know which she preferred. Ever since she turned thirteen, she wasn't sure. She was only sure she couldn't say no to her father.

At the shore, her father pushed the bowed, white rowboat aside, looping the ropes more tightly around the willow tree that shaded the water. Then he stepped into the lake. Jennifer watched his feet sink into the spongy, mucky bottom, the decaying weeds oozing up around his toes like an octopus. The thought of stepping in it made her suck in a deep breath. Her father looked at her.

"Not getting cold feet, are you, Jenny?"

"No," Jennifer said, quite clearly, she thought, and she dipped her foot into the ooze. Her father was already up to his waist.

"We'll just go to the island, unless you have so much energy left you want to swim across to the other side." The water closed around his chest and he pushed into a swimming position. His thin, muscly arms picking up an even, neat stroke, as his head rolled evenly, catching deep breaths as it rocked. Jenny could already hear his rhythm. She looked across the water to the wooded island, sitting plump and settled in the middle of the lake. Only to the island. She drew in a breath and pushed away from the weedy bottom.

Her strokes were short, pretty enough, but short, and she had never learned to "breathe properly," her father had told her, so she held her head up as she pulled across the water. One, two. One, two. Her feet kicked evenly. Her pace was steady enough, but even in the first moments, she could see her father begin to pull away.

That was all right.

Jenny looked back at the cottage for an instant. It was still there, a little smaller perhaps, white and boxlike, sitting on the sloped rise back from the bay. She caught sight of her mother, too, wiping her hands on her apron as she walked down toward the shore.

"Be careful, Jenny!" she called to her.

That was her mother, for certain, always urging, "Be careful, Jenny." One, two. One, two. Jenny wondered if all mothers closed all conversations that way. Like some people said "good-bye" or "have a nice day." It was a pull, really, a father who said "let's try . . ." and a mother who said "be careful." Bla, bla, bla.

The water had felt icy at first, but now it felt mellow, amber like its color, except now and then when Jenny's flutter-kick fluttered too deep and caught some icy stream. Some surprise beneath. Mostly it felt sun-warmed. One, two. And there were no waves. One, two. One, two. Jennifer turned over on her back and caught the sun on her face. Small gnats danced in the air above the quiet water. It was almost restful enough to go to sleep. Jennifer smiled. She had been uneasy about swimming to the island, and now she was thinking about going to sleep.

She stretched her arms back, kicking evenly. How long had she been swimming? Five minutes? Ten? Time was so elusive out here, but what did it matter? She was making it. She turned over, a little surprised to find her father pulling even farther ahead. She could only see his head, his hair wet and shiny in the sun, dipping evenly between the stroking arms.

A catch of panic. But she wasn't tired. Not really. The crawl was a little hard to keep up since she had to toss her head from side to side, but there were other strokes that would get her there. Jennifer snapped her legs together, then coasted for a minute to rest. When she started to kick again, she tried the scissors kick with a sidestroke. That felt better. She stretched into the sidestroke. Easily. Relaxed. What did it matter that he was so far ahead? She was making it alone. One, two. One, two.

A slight wind had begun to pick up the waves, and a ripple edged across the water, lapping at Jennifer's face, splashing gently at her head. One . . . two. Perhaps it was better not to try to think. Suddenly that seemed to require energy. Jennifer switched into an extended dog paddle. That was a sloppy stroke, her father had said, but it wouldn't hurt. She just wanted to see where they were. Her father was just a bobbin in the waves now, way ahead. More than halfway to the island. Jenny took a deep breath, the best she could, then turned on her side again. Her arms had become too heavy for the crawl. Too heavy. She looked back at the shoreline. Her mother was standing there, her hands still wrapped in her apron. It was nearly as far back as it was to the island. Jennifer caught her breath and blew out deeply. Again and again.

If only she could rest for a moment, she could start again, but suddenly she realized (of course, she must have known it all along) that there was nothing to rest on. Nothing! Probably Joey didn't need a rest stop. Probably. Her father didn't need one; his stroke was pulling him like a tiny machine toward the island. But Jennifer knew her arms were getting heavier, heavier. Of course, that was impossible. Still, it was so. It was so.

She looked back again. "Back" looked so possible. Hadn't she come from there already? Well, then she could return. But then she had been fresh; now, she was heavy, sogged. Even her skin seemed to weigh. And her shoulders. And her hands. Yes, her hands and feet were the heaviest of all. They would barely move. Her breath cut deeply into her lungs. Perhaps she should call her father. No, then he would say he should have known she couldn't make it. That it was too far for her. Even if he didn't say it, that's what he would think.

Jennifer stopped entirely for a moment and treaded water, leaning slightly, restfully on her back. That helped. Why hadn't she thought of it before? Her head rocked gently with the waves, her long hair swirling around her neck. Yes, this is what she should have done long before.

After several minutes, then, she turned, ready again, almost ready for the crawl. Yet, to be sensible, she started off with the sidestroke. Evenly. Scissor, pull. Scissor, pull. One, two. One, two. But the icy air caught at her lungs after only a few yards, and the heaviness returned, even more heavily. And her arms could not reach ahead. Not a single stroke. And she heard herself call to the bobbing head.

"Dad! Dad!" It was a frightened voice.

The head turned around. "What?" His voice was so far away.

"I'm tired!"

"Just tread water for a minute," he yelled.

"I can't anymore."

Was he annoyed when he turned? She couldn't tell, but she heard him. "All right. All right. Keep treading. I'm coming."

And she felt less tired just seeing him come. Even though he wasn't a tree. Or a boat. He was her Dad, and strong enough somehow.

As she watched him swim, still evenly toward her, she thought she saw a hint of disappointment. Or perhaps he was just blowing some water off of his face. That was it. He was just shaking water off.

Then he was next to her.

"Now," he said, glancing at the shoreline briefly, "hold on to my shoulder. Lightly. Because if you pull me down, neither of us will get there. Lightly. That's it."

She touched him so lightly, his strong, browned shoulders, and she kicked and he kicked. She could see that the island was really only fifty yards or so ahead, in all its fringed plumpness. Larger now. Much closer than the shore had been. She really had forgotten to look ahead.

And she wished he would say something to her. Something like, that's all right, Jennifer. It's a long swim and you did fine. But she knew he was tired; that's why he didn't say those things. That really was why.

But even as they swam comfortably for minutes, he still said nothing, and suddenly Jennifer knew she had to push away from him. And she started to stroke next to him, tiredly but surely. She knew she would make the island from here.

Part Two

IT'S STRANGE. I feel as if the train is running faster. That's silly. It's probably set by computers — all the same speed. But I feel that way. I didn't at first. Even though I could feel the wheels, I knew the towns were doing the racing, the farmhouses, the hills. Not me. But it's ten o'clock at night and I'm beginning to feel like we're racing, too, all of us. This train, the soldier, the gray-haired lady, the attendant, me. Maybe it's the night lights streaking by. Or the station signs ticking off Maysville, Huntington. Or the people getting on and getting off. They're always the clue.

Maybe it's just my waiting, and knowing there's only seven more hours left to think anything over. To put words together, even though I know that's silly. When there are two people that have to say something to each other, two people have to figure out the words. To know the right ones.

That man in the beige suit across the aisle isn't worried about words. He doesn't seem to feel the wheels racing. Not the way he's watching me. Probably thinks I'm 24, or he's hoping. I wonder when it changes. When men start looking at a girl more like a woman and less like a daughter. I remember the pharmacist, Bob, at the drugstore always grumping at me: "Please, don't lean on the comic books." "Careful, you're fingering the Clark bars." "If you're not going to buy that *Mad* magazine, don't open it." Bla, bla, bla, and always through those foggy glasses, which I could see were staring somewhere else anyway. Then last year when I was sixteen, there was Bob, asking, "You're the Cooper girl, aren't you? All growed up." Oh, that is funny. "Growed up," he says, ogling, steaming his four-inch thick glasses.

"Growed up" has got to mean more than being able to fit into a 36 bra. It really has to. What is the sign, I wonder? It can't be age. When I was ten I could hardly wait to be twelve because twelve was "growed up." But when I was twelve I was convinced fourteen was the magic number . . . until I stumbled into fourteen; then I hoped it was fifteen . . . or sixteen. But here I am seventeen and still waiting. Waiting. Maybe it's like walking through a string of cars on a night train. You're there — "growed up" — when you can walk without stumbling, without the wind catching you between cars or the motion taking you. Maybe it's just when you finally know the right words.

One thing is certain, it all adds up. Meanwhile we wait and wait like I am now, always expecting something tomorrow.

J ENNIFER HELD HER NOSE. The boards reeked
of days and months of wet bathing suits thrown on the
seats and floors. With the other hand she pulled on the bottom of her bikini, looking quickly at the seam in the wood.
There was the old story about the boys finding the hole in
the wall between the boys' and girls' changing rooms.
Probably it was this room. Just her luck.

"Are you nearly ready?" a voice called from outside the
room.

"Almost." Jennifer quickly pulled on the suit and
slipped into the bra top. Most kids changed together,
walking around naked, throwing their suits on. Jenny did,
too, when she was ten. Even twelve. But when she turned
thirteen, there were new problems. Like where to look
when your friends undressed with you and you realized
their bodies were getting soft and round, they were getting brown-tipped breasts, and you still looked like your
ten-year-old cousin. The only things that stuck out were
your ribs.

"What is *almost*? There won't be any good spots left on
the beach!" Sue called. It was more than that. Jenny knew.

"Da-dah!" Jennifer jumped out of the curtain with a
fanfare.

"All right." Sue smiled. "Let's go."

They weren't so far apart in age, only a year, but something was happening to Sue. Something Jennifer couldn't put her finger on. Always before they had wanted to do the same things. Swim at the park. Walk up and down the nearby street of big Victorian houses, saying they were thirsty and could they have a drink or they were studying architecture and could they please see the insides of the sprawling clapboard houses.

Sue had other things on her mind this summer.

The park grass, which ran nearly down to the sand, was covered with flags of towels thrown down at angles, a cacophony of transistor stations, bodies, brown or browning, sleeping, on elbows talking, or backs baking. Jennifer balanced her way through the maze, finding the tufts of grass which meant free passage.

Sue went first, talking, swinging her arms and casually stepping where she had to, a toe into someone's suntan lotion, her towel dragging across someone's arm. At ease with the sun beaming down on her blond curly hair, her already bronzed back. Knowing there would be a place for her.

Close to the sand's edge, she took a body-length spot surrounded by empty towels and flipped them back to make a place for two.

"This looks good," she said, not really looking at Jenny when she said it, but pulling her lotion out of her big, floppy purse and pouring some into her hand, which she stroked over her arms as if she were soaping herself in the bathtub.

Jennifer took the bottle from her extended hand and did

the same. She knew Sue was waiting for something. No, it was more than that. Sue was waiting for someone. Maybe more than one. Jennifer was, too, but it was as if Sue knew what she was waiting for — Jennifer only guessed. It made her feel uneasy. Always before she had been the one to go up to the Victorian mansion to ask for water, but this was different. She smiled to herself. Maybe if she had more than a rib cage to fill out her bathing suit.

"What are you smiling at?" Sue asked without looking.

"An inside joke," Jennifer answered. She turned over to let her back side take the baking.

"I saw Bill Sorenson and Jack Jones here yesterday."

"Did you talk to them?" Jenny asked. The boys were ninth-graders. Since the sixth grade Jenny had really barely spoken to boys in her own grade, let alone a ninth-grader.

"Of course! We talked about Jack working for his father all summer. And Bill was talking about some party." Sue was stroking her arms and looking over the lawn.

Jennifer had never been to a boy-girl party, well, only two. One was her own. But both parties had been in the sixth grade with kids she had grown up with from kindergarten. Marian Lindquist. Ann Armstrong. That whole group. On a dare Duane Wilson had had to kiss her. Yuk. Jimmy Anderson had held her arms in back of her.

Jennifer shuddered and put her head down on the towel. It felt scratchy against her cheek, but the sun felt warm and softening on her other cheek and her hair. Almost as if she weren't waiting.

"Honestly, I don't think there will be anyone here today. Dull. Dull." Sue breathed out a bored sigh and turned over on her stomach, clicking her radio to a station whining with blues-blended rock.

Even talking about it didn't help. Jennifer could feel the sun's heat move slowly across her body, now warming her shoulders, now the backs of her legs. Nothing was happening. Whatever it was they were waiting for, it wasn't happening.

But when Sue sat up to go for a swim, four boys near the refreshment stand called to her.

"Hey, look-it here! Sue! Look what we've got."

Sue folded her legs under her and got up gracefully. "Come on, Jen," she whispered, suddenly smiling. "It's Bill Sorenson."

Jenny pushed back her hair and followed more slowly. She was suddenly aware of all her parts and wondered how they were working on their own. Aware there was no hiding them in a bathing suit.

Sue walked up to Bill and playfully punched his thick, tanned arm. "Hey!" she said.

"Hey, yourself," he smiled, his teeth painfully white in his dark face.

Jennifer stepped up behind Sue, trying to belong. Trying to stand straighter. Trying to shake her hair back out of her eyes. But saying nothing.

"Look, what we've got here. A present," Bill was saying.

Only after a moment or so did Jennifer see what they had. In the grass lay a gull, a large gray and white streaked gull, whose one wing was spread out, dragging behind him.

"Oh, poor thing," Sue said. She kneeled next to it. Gulls were common along the lake shore, and out along the concrete breakwater that surrounded the swimming area. Not here, ten feet from the refreshment stand.

"What can we do for it?" As she tried to touch it, it took a frantic leap, flapping and tottering like a drunken sailor.

Amused, a dark-haired boy took a stick and nudged its tail again. The bird flopped over helplessly, his wing dragging alongside of him. "He's no airplane. That's for sure. He's a clown!"

Sue laughed. "Oh, come on, Charlie. Don't be so mean."

Jennifer could feel herself growing warm.

Sue grabbed the stick playfully away from the boy. "You're awful, really awful."

Another boy, tall, with a cup of lemonade in his one hand, kneeled down and looked at the gull. "A gull with a broken wing can't last. I'll just dump it over in the bushes. He's probably diseased."

"Over there near the fence," another girl said, taking off her sunglasses to look more closely. Two toddlers came up, inches from the bird and poked at it with their fingers, and pleased with the way the gull jumped, did it again. Giggling.

Jennifer knew she would have to stop it.

"No," she said. "I'll take it home." She set out her lip determinedly and tried gently, carefully to move the bird out of the reach of the children.

Sue looked at her, puzzled. The two boys laughed. "Oh, come on! How ?"

"Jennifer!" Sue's smile was threatening.

"I'm not letting it be dumped in the bushes. I'm not." Jennifer was stroking the gull's head. "It's only his wing. Other animals recover. Don't they? Don't they?" For the first time she looked up at the three boys defiantly. She could feel the tears welling up in her, but she was determined they wouldn't see them. And they wouldn't take the bird away from her.

"It's pretty stupid, if you ask me. It's just an old gull," the girl with glasses said. "He's probably crippled from old age."

The boys all laughed.

Jennifer could feel her face grow red, but she kept stroking the gull's head. The bird had stopped flapping. What if it were an old gull? Or a really sick one? Maybe she couldn't heal the wing, but she could set the bird somwhere by the lake, away from people. She wasn't just being stupid. Jennifer looked down at the gull, hunched over on its side, breathing heavily but quiet. She felt such a sense of anger for it, but she felt the boys' dislike of her, too.

"Look, I'll get rid of it. You don't have to know where we put it." It was Bill Sorenson. His thick hands were reaching over her shoulders.

Jenny blocked his hand.

"No," she said stubbornly.

Obviously annoyed, he started to brush her shoulder aside.

But Sue came up next to Jenny. "Wait." She put her hand in between the boy and Jennifer. "We'll take it to my house; it's close. Maybe we can do something . Come on, Jenny. Let's get changed."

Jenny just sat, stroking the feathered head.

The boys shrugged and started away.

Jennifer felt an emptiness. Whatever she and Sue had

been waiting for was over. There was no chance it would come back again. Not today. She turned. The boys were walking out on the pier, sauntering, laughing. Having already forgotten.

"I'm sorry, Sue. I just couldn't let them do that," she said.

Sue didn't answer. She was slipping her tight pink skirt over her suit. "For God's sake, Jenny. Let's just get a box and stop talking about it. OK?"

And Jenny went over to the refreshment stand, slowly, feeling empty, but not knowing why.

JENNIFER STEPPED into the tack room behind the graying man. She wondered how his jeans stayed on his skinny hips at all, but they moved right with him, part of him, blue and dusty, clinging to his hips and his rumpled brown plaid shirt. On the walls of the tiny room bridles and halters were hung on hooks. The smell of leather made Jennifer heady. Excited. The man fingered one bridle, thought for a moment, then went on to a second one.

"You only ride once before?" he asked over his shoulder.

"Just once. When I was eight or nine."

"That's like nothing," he muttered, slipping a scuffed set

of the leather strips off a third hook, "but if you just walk Danny, he'll do good for you." The man's Adam's apple moved comfortably up and down as he talked to Jennifer, and she found herself nodding and following him into the stable.

But at the door he turned, and pointed to a spot on the floor just outside the tack room. "Just stay here," he said. "I'll get him."

Two single bulbs hung from the ceiling, not really lighting the narrow stalls that strung across the two sides. Piles of manure were kicked up toward the backs of the stalls, some still steaming. The rumps of the animals moved, great round mountains of muscles, as the horses shifted their weight from one foot to the other. One shorter rump backed up, only to be stopped by the rope that cordoned off its stall. And there were shadowy sounds. A grumbling snort. A breathing stretch. Hooves shifting in the hay.

Jennifer stretched a little farther into the stable, trying not to overstep the point at which the hand had ordered her to "stay there," wondering what he would bring her. But she couldn't see him.

When she finally did, he was leading a tall, brown horse, a chestnut, who was pulling stubbornly away from the rope. "All right, Danny boy, nice and easy," he was saying. Jenny looked up at the horse's head as the man took the bridle and pulled it over its ears. She hadn't remembered that horses stood so tall. Not that tall.

"He uses an English saddle," the stable hand said. He flipped a Y-shaped saddle over the horse's back and cinched it. "Danny used to be 'shown' before he came here."

Jennifer stared up at the gigantic head; the deep brown liquid eyes shifted uneasily.

"Sometimes he's stubborn, but mostly he's just too old to care. Eh, Dan?" the hand said, holding the silver stirrup out for Jennifer to mount.

Jennifer wasn't even sure which foot went in the stirrup, but before she could guess, the man tapped her left knee. "That one," he said, with undisguised disgust.

Jennifer put her toe into the stirrup and threw her leg over, settling comfortably into the brown leather seat. He handed her a double rein, then wove the leather strips between her third and fourth fingers. "Keep them taut, but not too taut. Sit back and relax. Danny's like an old car. He's not going far and he's not going fast." He was leading Jennifer past four boys waiting for horses. "Try the ring first."

The dusty path led to a peeling white slatted ring. Danny plugged toward it, head down, bobbing lazily with each step. Jennifer sat, wondering at the strange leather strips in her hands that didn't seem to be doing anything. She already felt better. Easier. Danny even turned into the gateway without Jennifer giving any direction. He started plugging, scuffling around the fall-hardened circle.

Two young girls were trotting in tandem around the ring, sitting straight on prim gray ponies, whose hooves seemed only to tap the ground as they rode out their rhythms. Carousel ponies. Even. Crisp. Jennifer watched them pass a second time, as Danny scuffled around the far side of the ring. Jennifer liked it this way. Nice and easy. And predictable.

When the two girls came to the gate on the third time around, one girl reached over, opened the gate, and trotted her pony out, leaving the gate ajar. As Danny came toward it, his ears pricked and he started to half trot, pulling Jennifer off balance. She fell forward and the reins flopped between her fingers.

"He's just thinking of getting back to the stable! Don't let him!" the hand shouted at her as he led some horses out. "Just sit back and get him past that gate."

But Jennifer couldn't. She was too scared. She knew it. She felt her feet flopping out of the stirrups as Danny started to trot faster.

"Sit back!" the man shouted angrily. "For God's sake. *Sit* back!"

Suddenly Jennifer was too scared not to. She pulled herself back a little.

"Tuck your butt under!" he shouted again.

Jennifer tried.

"And hold that rein just taut. Not tight!" The man was at the gate watching her.

God, Jennifer tried, and miraculously she felt the horse pull up and even out his trot. At the gate, Jennifer held her seat and kept the reins firm. The horse's head started to turn toward it. She pulled at the opposite rein and he went straight . . . past the gate.

"Now, you're talking," the man shouted, and Jennifer somehow felt kindly toward him, in spite of his scratchy voice. "All right, now take him around a few times. Then you can walk him on the trail if you'd like. *Walk him*! I said!"

Jennifer brought Danny back to a walk and after a few more circles decided they knew each other well enough to go out on the trail. She didn't feel apart from him as she had at first. They'd just walk.

The trail was rutted and ridged into dried hoof scuffs. It

had rained last week And dried. Trees crowded the trail; stones, pushed to the sides, lined it as it wound its way in turns through the woods. It was a fall-crisp day — an airy day. Jennifer settled down into the warm leather, feeling her legs close against Danny's side, feeling her hips move as Danny's did in slow, lumbering paces. The reins lay loose in her hands. She could even look around through the spindly trees, naked now from last week's rain and wind storm, at the fallen leaves cradled against stumps and rocks. Probably she would see a deer. Or a ground-hog. Jennifer felt free, yet a part of Danny.

They could trot; she knew it. And on the moment Jennifer pulled her ankles into his sides. Nice and easy. Danny went on plugging. Jennifer pulled her ankles in again and clicked, and Danny started to trot. At first slowly, barely beyond walking, but trotting. Nice and steady. Clopping like some other time, finding the level spots on the lane, turning, wending his way through the tunnel of trees. Nice and steady. The two of them. Jennifer smelled the mix of Danny and the fall and she felt good, just trotting.

Then in back of her she heard voices and a quicker thudding of hooves. People were riding up behind her, and for some reason which she didn't try to understand, she felt herself grow tight. She sat back ("Just sit back!") and tried to bring Danny down to a walk.

But the hooves were getting closer, and Danny's ears turned around like antennae. Jennifer could feel his spine arch under her and his trot quicken. And she grew even tighter and pulled back harder on the reins.

The horses behind her were catching up, cantering, not so fast, but the riders were shouting above the hooves and laughing. "On your right!" one shouted as he rode up behind her, but as he passed, Danny suddenly gave a little hop, then broke, bursting down the lane after them.

At first it was an easy canter, almost easier than the trot, but as the riders stretched out ahead, Danny wanted to win. Jennifer could feel it. She tried to tug at the reins, but he just pulled against them flying after the others. ("Sit back! Sit back!") And suddenly Jenny felt his motion, not cantering — flying, swallowing the road, and she stood up in her stirrups, leaning over the saddle, leaning over his mane and let him fly. And she was on him and she was him, gathering up the road, swallowing it, the trees spinning by, and suddenly, passing the other horses, leaving them behind.

They flew. And flew.

And where the path took an angled sweep around a pasture, Danny slowed, and feeling it, Jennifer pulled lightly on the rein, touched it, and sat back ("Get your butt under!") and felt Danny drop back to a canter, then a trot, and finally a walk, heaving deep breaths as his head bobbed wearily from side to side with each step.

Back at the stable, Jennifer's knees nearly folded under her when she swung her legs back to the ground.

"Well, old Danny bore you to death?" the man said, his Adam's apple rising and falling, easy, sure of her answer.

Jennifer smiled.

"Next time you can have something better," he assured her, leading old Danny into the darkened, bulb-lit stable.

"GRANDMA."

"Yes, Jennifer."

"About Great Aunt Harriet."

"Yes, Jenny."

"She never married, ever."

"That's right."

"Did she ever want to get married?"

"Not that I know of, Jenny."

"Did she ever go out with a boy . . . or a man?"

"I'm not really sure, Jenny."

"Did she ever talk to a boy?"

"Well . . . I recall she was friendly with her cousin John's friends."

(pause)

"She's been *alone* all these years . . . fifty years, I bet. More. Wearing those silky dresses down to her ankles and her hair back in a bun. Did she always look like that?"

"Harriet was not unattractive, Jen, no mistaken that. And she has not been exactly alone. She has lots of friends. And don't you forget she has a fine job. She's an auditor."

(pause)

"You know what I think?"

"What?"

"I think there are girls . . . women . . . who probably never talk to a boy. Never kiss a boy. Never. And they dry up and wear their hair in buns and wear long silky dresses to their ankles."

"Jenny, Jenny. Patience."

"Probably Great Aunt Harriet runs in the family!"

CHRISTOPHER MICHAEL COCHRAN. She took the pencil and pulled the point carefully over the pages of her book until the letters stood proudly and rather neatly on the edges. Christopher Michael Cochran. Then she set the book down on her desk, its edges toward the windows, and looked at Mrs. Turner.

Not that she had courage. She couldn't even tell Mrs. Turner where the Caucasus Mountains lay. Or the River Ob. Or the Caspian Sea. Well, not out loud anyway. Not like Alice Richards could. Jenny looked at the head in front of her, bent over, the long brown hair, thick and wavy, falling over the girl's face. Alice always-doing-the-right-thing Richards. Now, busily working on her map. In five minutes writing in her perfectly formed penmanship a perfectly correct test. Smiling in twenty minutes, well, twenty-one minutes, at Tommy Hyland and Johnny Etchworth, chatting about hockey. Or basketball. Or whatever.

"Well, the Red Wings were really super Sunday night. I just couldn't go to bed without hearing what happened to Ravelle," she would say, shaking her head with great interest.

"Fantastic," Tommy and Johnny would answer in unison. "I swear," Tommy would go on, "You *said* they were going to beat Montreal. I never figured it that way."

Jenny shuddered. Perfection. Her mother was right; no one deserved to reach polished, neated-up perfection at the age of fourteen. That was ridiculous. Jenny smiled to herself. It would be more perfect if Alice had one bad day, and, oh, how Jenny wanted to see it.

First, the maps. Let Alice put the Caspian Sea in the Great Lakes. More, more, Alice. Assert with great authority to Mrs. Turner that Schenectady is in Saudi Arabia. That the Gulf of Mexico surrounds Iceland. Then after class, let it roll down on you, Lady Alice.

"The Red Wings were fantastic last night," say, with a shake of your brown locks.

"Oh?" Tommy and Johnny may say in unison. "The Red Wings didn't play last night. They're doing a basketball benefit in Kansas City."

Jenny put her head down on the desk and looked sideways toward the windows. All thoughts of ever locating the Caspian Sea without her book had left her. If she needed to rent a boat there, she'd find it. She was looking at a blond, curly-haired boy, who, catching her looking at him, turned away, his cheeks reddening instantly.

Jenny looked away, feeling heat in her own cheeks.

They had been looking at each other like this for over three weeks. Late bloomers. Oh, that dreadful phrase. A euphemism, her aunt said, for being flat chested or shy and/or both. Jenny stared into a sort of blur, still seeing him out of the corner of her eye. Of course, it could all be in her mind.

Slowly, posing her pen in hand, as if she were in full action, she went over things again. Maybe everything was in her mind. The possibility made her cover the edges of her book self-consciously. Let's see. Three weeks ago, when Mrs. Turner had asked for everybody to break down into groups he, Christopher Michael Cochran, had come over and sat behind her when the class was counting off in twos. And that week when they worked on the relief map and she had plopped down a handful of mud for the mountains in Egypt instead of India, he had taken another handful and, placing the gob in Iowa, had said, "If Egypt can use some more mountains, so can Iowa. It will help break up the scenery." Jenny hid a laugh in her hands. When Mrs. Turner had seen the misplaced mountains, she had said to them both, "We're not creating a new world, you two; we're trying to get an idea of the old one." Jennifer had felt so close in that conspiracy. But after that week he had never waited for her after class or anything.

It made her a little empty to think. One day he had even joined Tommy and Johnny and discussed, yuk, hockey, with Alice Richards.

But there was last week. He had passed that note to her. She knew it by heart. "Jenny Cooper, girl geographer;

how's Egypt these days? Sighted any new mountain chains?" He hadn't had to write that note. It was a little insane. And he did smile, even though he looked straight ahead, when she wrote back: "Haven't been to Egypt lately. Got stuck in Iowa, looking at the scenery." Smile, straight ahead.

Tick. Tick. The school clock was black and white and persistent, but not easily pushed around. Somehow today she wanted it to slow down. She wanted its fat, fed face to lumber to 2:03. Not to hurry there. Had he seen the letters on her book? Had he seen her glance at him? Had he seen her cheeks grow pink?"

Oh, and there was that time in the hall Wednesday. That seemed important, too, when she was remembering. Marguerite "Cheerleader" Smith had practically pushed Jenny over, trying to get her books out of her locker so she could get to practice. But Jenny didn't hurry with her lower locker. All right, she wasn't a cheerleader. All right, she liked to swim lengths in a pool and not race against anyone and not go out after school for basketball but to go home and listen to records and write in her journal and sometimes play with the kids next door. Play "Red Rover, Red Rover" on spring days when all the kids swelled out of their houses like the high tide. How could Marguerite "Cheerleader" Smith know about the feel of making a line across Buckingham Street and staring into the faces of another line of kids who had sometimes been your friends, but were right now your arch enemies? How could she know the feeling of digging your sneakers into the asphalt and gripping your teeth and shouting, "Red Rover, Red Rover, let Peter come over!" and seeing the kid come tear-ing at your arms? And the look you gave Patsy Miller, next to you, when your arms and hers held and Peter had to return alone to his own line. Red Rover. Red Rover.

What had Chris said when Marguerite pushed Jenny aside?

"Hey, Cheerleader, you trying out for the football team?"

Jenny looked harder straight ahead. Maybe he hadn't meant anything by it. Maybe he hadn't meant that Marguerite had been a little rough on Jenny. Maybe it was just a way for him to talk to Marguerite. Jenny felt her face flush again. Darn face. It just wouldn't let her have her secrets. She felt her fingers creep tightly over the letters on the side of the book. Maybe it all came to nothing. Maybe Jenny had just waited so long to talk to a boy, really talk to one, that she had blown this whole Chris thing into something it wasn't.

Jenny filled her chest with air and closed her eyes. That probably was it. She had dreamed up something that wasn't. Again. Slowly, she looked down at the paper and started to concentrate on Russia. But it wasn't easy. Truly it wasn't. Not with him over there. And her feeling him the way she did. Kiev, here. Leningrad, here. Moscow . . .

Alice never raised her head. Marguerite never stopped smiling. Tommy and Johnny never stopped thinking about hockey. And waiting. Everyone seemed routed into grooves like a 33 rpm record. Already grooved. Spinning. There really was no place to climb on. So you waited. Waited until someone came to you. Pulled you onto the spinning thing. Or maybe stopped spinning long enough to walk quietly in a straight line. Strange, that sounded like the path everyone would take. But it wasn't; the spinning path was the one they all took — like cartoon characters set in motion, well planned, predictable, round and round, looking at each other. Alice, Marguerite, Tommy, Johnny, Alice, Marguerite, Tom . . .

Chris? She wasn't sure. All she knew was he played the drums sometimes. And sometimes he played baseball. And swam. And sometimes he built mountains.

The clock read 2:03 and the bell bleated. No note. Not today. No recognition that he had seen his name. Tomorrow seemed like such a long way away, more like a year, five years.

Jenny picked up her books slowly. Maybe, if she waited until everyone was gone. Mrs. Turner was gathering her brown notebook, the one with the lesson plans and marks, and smiling at Bill McCaffery, who was teasing her about wearing a Waterbury High sweatshirt. Jim Follin was stacking his papers, so none of them would stick out further than the others, and clicking his tongue at his inefficiency. He was taking forever. But Chris was still there, too.

Jenny dropped her pencil. That would take a minute. She pulled up her stockings while she was bent over. She could see Chris beginning to start up the aisle. He hadn't come over. A cold, horrible emptiness swelled in her. It would be another day then. And maybe she was waiting for nothing.

Quickly, she gathered her papers, sticking them this way and that, looking more than a little windswept, though the air was horribly still. Her blouse hanging out of her skirt, one strand of hair falling nearly over her eye, she blew it up and started out of the room. She'd never make Science on time now.

Then, as she turned the corner, the notebook slipped. Papers tumbled out of arms, between arms, into the center of the feet-scrambled corridor. She sucked up a draft of air, ready to attack the mess, when she felt fingers on her arm.

"Hey, that's what you get for mountain watching. Your head's not on right!" Jenny looked up uneasily at the grinning blond-haired boy. After all, it had all been a dream. "I take that back," he said to her, picking up a dog-eared science book just before it was kicked. "Your head's OK."

Oh, Christopher Michael Cochran, so's yours.

❈▱❈▱❈▱❈▱❈▱❈▱❈▱❈▱❈▱❈▱❈

"Jenny!"

"Yes, Dad. I can't hear you."

"I said, that's enough shower for today!"

"Oh!"

"Jennifer, do you hear me?"

"What, Dad?"

"I said get out of the shower! You're using water as if it were free."

"I'll be out soon, Dad."

"But you took a shower this morning!"

"What, Dad?"

"I said, YOU TOOK A SHOWER THIS MORN-ING!"

"I didn't wash my hair this morning!"

"Do you have to wash your hair every day?"

"What?"

"DO YOU HAVE TO WASH YOUR HAIR EVERY DAY?"

"YES!"

"This is ridiculous. No human being needs to be that clean!"

"What?"

"I said . . . NO HUMAN . . . hell, I said . . . JENNY GET OUT OF THE SHOWER! NOW!"

"WELL," THE BOY SAID, slapping mustard on a plain piece of bread, "I say we should go any-way."

Jenny watched him and shook her head. How a friend of hers could eat a bologna sandwich with mustard and not butter was mind-boggling. "Have you ever tried but-ter with bologna?" she coaxed.

Christopher Michael Cochran looked up at her and

twisted his entire face into a frown. "Will you stop trying to convert me? I say we should go to the beach anyway. The clouds don't look that serious to me."

It was hard to concentrate on making a decision when there was the bologna to think about, and Mrs. Cochran in the very next room, probably thinking how strange it was to have a fourteen-year-old girl for lunch at her house. Maybe she wasn't thinking that at all. Jenny grinned to herself. Maybe it only seemed strange to Jenny. Not only having him all to herself sitting across from her like . . . well, like an old friend, but smelling all the Chris smells, so different from any she had smelled.

The kitchen had a day-old bacon smell, and beyond that, was it a furniture polish smell from the dining room? It smelled like her great Aunt Lucy's Victorian sitting parlor. Oh, and there was the cat smell of ornery Fritzie, the Fritzie that Chris had talked so much about, now rubbing moodily across her legs. It was all so strange and familiar.

"Look, Jenny, we've got to decide. Enough about this bologna business. I refuse to eat butter on my sandwich. It's a matter of principle." He chomped off a half-a-sandwich-sized bite and looked up.

Jenny smiled and shook her head. She almost told him he should take smaller bites, but suddenly knowing that came out of her father's table script, she thumped down her fist.

"I say, you're right," she said dramatically. "Butter is not necessary and, yes, clouds are bound to pass."

He reached across the table and squeezed her arm. She still hadn't really gotten used to his touching her. It always startled her. Just the touch.

And the feeling it gave her still made her a little shaky when she followed him out the back door to the garage into the hot, cloud-heavy July day. But she didn't let on.

"All right, I'll ride you on my bicycle bar. If it gets too rough, we can walk awhile. I told John Etchworth we'd be at the park at two o'clock." Chris pulled off his tee shirt and brushed it up into his blond hair to wipe off the sweat that had already beaded on his forehead. His shoulders were not wide, but his browned skin had waves of muscles.

Jenny watched him drag out a spindly, repainted gray bicycle, dust off the seat, then swing his leg over. Satisfied, he released his one hand from the bars and motioned.

"Come on, come on, slowpoke."

"You'd be a slowpoke, too, if you felt like you were taking your life into your hands. I'm generally careful about my mode of transportation, you know."

Chris shook his head at "mode of transportation." They had only been seeing each other for a few weeks, but he already had a stock response for her four-syllable words: he shook his head and proclaimed, like now, "Nut."

Jenny wrinkled her nose at him and with pretended haughtiness sat up on the bar. As Chris started down the two-strip driveway, the bike teetered.

"Chris!" Jenny demanded.

"Now, now, just building your character. Want to see if you can take it." He swerved to the other track, and Jenny closed her eyes. The sudden vision of her toppled over in the rosebush was starkly real.

But then with a glide they were down the driveway and into the wide street, spinning past rows of cars parked in front of houses that were really four houses in one. The trunks of the heavy, leafy oak trees squeezed into the narrow strips between sidewalks and streets, their boughs bending over the street, touching tentatively in the middle.

It always made the road dark, but today, with the umbrella of swollen clouds, it was almost like nightfall. Jenny settled back against Chris's bare chest. It made her feel more secure, and his smell was so good. It was some sort of soap and the best smell she ever remembered smelling. She wished she could tell him.

Her wondering almost made her miss the faint thundering that rumbled back behind the houses. But then the leaves of the trees above them started to move restlessly, and Jenny could feel the wind nudge the lightweight bike over toward the parked cars. Chris compensated by bicycling faster. Jenny sat a little more upright but didn't say anything. There was a spark of lightning that lighted up the road. Then as they turned on a boulevard, a crash of thunder rolled out over the trees. Chris bicycled faster.

More thunder.

A spatter of rain hit Jenny's knee, then her chin. She looked at him.

"Hmmmm," she purred.

"I didn't say it *wouldn't* rain, you know." And in midsentence the rain started falling in sweeping, gusty sheets. "I only said — " and he had to raise his voice above the rain to be heard " — that WE . . . SHOULD . . . GO . . . ANYWAY!"

Jenny nodded in deference to the booming thunder as Chris steered the bike to the side. At the curb he put his foot down so Jenny could climb off, got off himself, then led her, running, to a porch. A stranger's porch.

Jenny wiped the water off her face and looked down at herself. She was drenched and the white tee shirt clung to her small breasts. She pulled it away from her skin, but it slowly receded back to its sticky wetness. She pulled it out again.

Chris looked at her, his curly hair hanging in wet ringlets around his face and neck, and grinned at her predicament.

"Well," she said overseriously, "that is what I get for trusting a bologna-and-mustard man!"

And he laughed, and she laughed, all out of proportion to the joke. And he took her hand, something like she and her friend Mary used to do when they were five years old and wanted to be close in a crowd, and he pulled her close to him and put his face, wet and warm, against her face, wet and warm, and he kissed her.

And there was no thunder or sleeting rain, only that moment, that first moment, and the smell of soap, and he looked down at her and said.

"You know what's funny? You're my best friend, my very best friend."

And Jenny nodded and felt tears in her eyes because it was so for her, too.

Part Three

MORE WAITING. The train has stopped. I had gotten used to checking off the miles by the stations. Night empty, hollow, yellow bulbs lighting them, the attendant pacing, yelling, "All-aboard!" We're in the middle of a plowed up field outside of some town. It's quiet here. Dark. Something about a mailbag hook bent at the last station, whatever that means. Forty-minute delay.

I don't know if I like it or not. It's always: give me more time, give me more time. When I'm suddenly given more, I don't know if I want it. Sneakers in Seat 21 just took a sandwich out of her brown grocery bag, not bothered at all. The soldier merely turned over at the news. Seat 23, Beige Suit, is smiling at me again.

I wonder what he sees when he sees me. Maybe it's like looking at the color green. I've thought a lot about that. Once I was thumbing through a stack of paint chips my father forgot to return to some unsuspecting paint store when it occurred to me that probably no color ever looks the same to anyone. Brown is never just brown; blue, not blue.

I even tested the hypothesis. I gave a green chip to my mother. Words, I said to her, give me words to describe it,

Mom. "Well," she said, "it's an ugly crepe-paper color. I don't like it. It reminds me of the paper my mother used to hang on our basement rafters at Christmas and take down a year later, faded and musty." Dad? "Oh, I don't know. Green is green. Well . . . maybe, well, maybe it's like the green chlorine bottle I keep the linseed oil in." My Aunt Margaret: "Oh, it is a lovely green, not soft, but it has a fertility in it, a dimension which says spring to me. Yes, that's it. It has an earthiness to it. I like it."

I could hardly believe it was the same green. Maybe it never will be. So what about Seat 23 over there, sitting and waiting for the train to move, watching me. Of course, he doesn't know me. Even so, does he see what my mother sees? What Chris sees? What my grandmother used to see, or my grandfather? It has to be different from what my teachers see or my friend Nancy. It is the three-part mirror all over again, multiplied by hundreds. What is the real green of me?

⊗══⊗══⊗══⊗══⊗══⊗══⊗══⊗══⊗══⊗══⊗

JENNY PUT HER BOTTOM to the squat iron stove and felt the wood-burning warmth spread through her blue jeans to her self, but the front of her shivered, and her stocking feet curled themselves up to avoid the cold linoleum. Just the opposite of her Grandma Stokes' house, there was nothing as cold as Grandma and Grandpa Cooper's house in the morning. Nothing.

In the corner Grandpa Cooper's rocking chair already rocked evenly as he smoked his first cigar and looked out the frosted, low-silled window. It wasn't often Grandpa rocked so quietly. Almost as if he had something on his mind. But as Jennifer watched, he swallowed some smoke, then tapped his cheeks, releasing comforting circles into the frosty kitchen. Then he glanced at her and winked. Everything must be all right.

Grandma bustled behind Jenny, placing the speckled blue coffeepot on the back burner. Her hunched shoulders and tiny withered face reminded Jenny of an apple-lady doll she had once seen, all folded and wrinkled into a tender warmth with gingham apron. Lots of people said her grandma and grandpa were poor; that's why they lived in such an old, not-modern house with no central heat and a falling-down porch, but it was hard for Jenny to know what poor was. Grandma was always busy baking something or cutting potatoes for something or scrubbing the floor or brewing tea or reading the Bible, and life didn't seem poor. Not to Jenny.

"What I need is a Jenny next to me," Grandpa called out. Grandpa had said that for as long as Jenny could remember. Sometimes it meant he was ready to pull out his frayed and dusty "Pilgrim's Progress" book, which he kept hidden behind Grandma's Bible books. He'd open it, nice and slow, savoring each page, showing her how you could feel the print with your fingertips. The flowery, oversize "T," the "S," the "M." And sometimes he'd go down the list of names scrawled and fading in the front cover: George Cooper, wheelwright, born 1716, d. 1749; Sarah Cooper, b. 1718, d. 1762; John Cooper, and so on.

But most times he'd pull her up on his lap and start telling his own stories. About Uncle Tom Cooper who was a horse thief and so ornery and thick-necked that when they finally caught him and tried to hang him, he just dangled from the noose and laughed, so they had to let him go free. Or the story of his brother Arthur, who had come to America from England when Grandpa had, but had set off to make his fortune in Arizona, and the last Grandpa had heard from him was a mysterious message that said, "Found silver. Write soon." Or he'd sing a "Bonny Lass" song which sometimes Jenny suspected he made up, because the words changed all the time.

His stories weren't only for Jenny. He was a custodian at a swimming club, and Old Jack — that's what they called him — had stories for everyone who picked up a bathing suit. But since he was "let go" because he had reached seventy-five, he sometimes didn't talk so much as he used to, and it had been a long time since Jenny had been small enough to climb in his lap.

Jenny tried to capture one more sense of the stove's warmth; then she ran over to the chair next to him.

Grandpa suddenly stopped and looked at her overseriously.

"And what happened to Uncle Tom Cooper, that wretched horse thief?" he asked mischievously, squinting one eye.

"Hanged but not hanged," Jenny whispered in a stage whisper, curling an invisible mustache.

"And Hannah Cooper?"

"Outspelled her entire school, including the teacher, won a trip to France to see Napoleon, but met a handsome Frenchman instead and swam 'nekked' in the River Seine . . ." She knew her stories well.

"And Harvey Cooper?"

"Mischievous sort." Again the stage whisper. "Escaped to Ireland in the dead of night to avoid praising an Anglican king." She rolled her r's.

Her grandfather laughed and his face wrinkled into a delighted look that he seemed to keep just for her, and he shook his head.

"I can't trap you, can I?"

Jenny answered with a question. "And what happened to dear Arthur, brother of Jack?"

"Off he rode to Arizona, my dear, where there came only the mysterious message . . ."

And they said it together, "Found silver. Write soon." They both paused, conjuring the possibilities of this adventurer Arthur, undoubtedly sitting rich as a king somewhere, just waiting for someone in the family to write. Jenny was still smiling when she felt her grandfather's hand reach over for hers.

Years before his neck had been broken in an automobile accident, and his hands, though still useful, were set in a stiff, stretched sort of pose. Jenny looked at his hand, the nails rounded, two of the fingers brown from the years of cigarettes and cigars they had held.

"Jennifer Lynn, you look more like a German than a good, solid Englishman. But in your soul I know otherwise. We've been friends a long while, I'm thinking."

Friends. Jenny smiled.

"And because in a way you're me, I'm glad you know

how to fly. You know how to step into the faeries' circle, and you know how to step out."

Grandpa didn't usually get so serious. Maybe this was what he had on his mind when he was staring out the window. He really did want to say these things. She just nodded and looked into his eyes.

"And knowing how you can fly or step smartly or sit and ponder, like now, well, Jenny, somehow that makes me feel like I found silver." Then he released her hand, and as the moment passed, he reached in for another cigar, bit it off, and said with an elfish grin, "And I'm a long way from Arizona."

THE BOY STOOD with his elbow in his hand, his fist propped up against his cheek, his hip out, leaning on one foot. His arms and legs were a silky bronze, rippling with long muscles that seemed wedded somehow to the green striped tank-top shirt. He tapped his toe impatiently, not just a simple tap, but back and forth almost as if it were being choreographed. David Blake was thinking, and when David Blake was thinking, no one else said a word.

No one on the stage moved.

Not even Jennifer, who still had difficulty remaining in any one position longer than three minutes. The entire line of fourteen girls stood — legs apart, legs crossed, leg resting behind leg on toe, leg with heel across foot, a line of legs in various states of repose across the entire stage. Waiting.

David Blake was a senior, the same age as many of the girls, but he was choreographer of the spring show. He was in charge of all the dancing — in charge, and he was a hard taskmaster. Out of the fourteen sets of legs, only six would be chosen to be dancers. Six. And even as she stood waiting, listening to the auditorium clock tick hollowly, Jennifer wasn't sure why she had come for tryouts.

Five of the girls had been in last year's show. Denise Silverman danced with the state ballet company. Penny Smith was a gymnast, supple as a willow branch. And at the one school dance Jennifer had gone to, Gail Ashby was the girl everyone circled and clapped for. Clapped and clapped. Jennifer stole a quick glance down the line. They all looked like dancers — willowy, together, with graceful hands and legs that met where they were supposed to. Jennifer was still thin, her legs never met, and they were impossibly short. It was crazy to have come.

"All right, we'll take it from the third measure. 'I'm going to wash that man right out of my hair, out of my hair . . .' " He was pacing. "Then, shuffle, shuffle, back, back." He started easing himself into the dance, all suppleness, liquid, melting into the music.

"Now . . . let's see you go through that part. Alone this time. If I tap you, step forward. Whatever happens, it has been a good two weeks. Piano! Give them a four-bar lead-in. Dah. Dah, da, da . . ." He hummed along with the piano, waving his arm abstractly as he paced the floor, head down, waiting for the entrance. "All right, now . . ."

And the piano chinked out the bars, a trumpet came in, and Jennifer felt her legs moving mechanically, shuffle, shuffle.

"Smile, for God's sake; this is not a funeral," David shouted.

Shuffle, shuffle, smile, back, back; turn once, turn twice, smile.

"Loosen up, Smith! You're dancing like you've got a rod in your back. Turn, turn, ease to the right. Together. Ease to the left."

Loosen up, ease to the right, ease to the left. Jennifer tried to hear the music. Tried to let it seep into her, the way she did at home when she danced by the record player. Tried to float. Together, together. Get the rod out of her back. Hip, hip, turn.

"Stay loose!" He was stopped right in front of her.

Jennifer felt her neck sweating, her cheeks pink. The short hairs around her face were sticking against it. Her tights were hiking up. She could barely remember the step. She looked quickly at Denise Silverman's feet. Ah, leap, back, bend, turn. Leap, back, bend, turn. David walked past her. He walked past Denise.

He walked to Alice Richards and tapped her. She stepped, smiling, out of the line. Alice had made it. Five more spots.

Jennifer brought her eyes back, staring out at the empty auditorium. She couldn't hesitate. Step, step, back together, back together. Wash that man. Wash that man.

David stood in front of Lois and tapped her. Jennifer felt her breath caught shallowly in her. That was a surprise, Lois making it. But there was still time.

Jennifer swung around, her long hair twisting around her shoulders. When she had turned back, Donna and Emily and Lois had stepped forward. One more to go. The line stared straight ahead, smiled stiffly, did a leap, sat, another leap, bend. Jennifer could barely hear the music. Then David went up to Penny and tapped her. She stepped forward and he sat back on the edge of the stage, waiting out the music.

It was over. So, all right, Jennifer had not made things before. She looked down the line, now filled with six empty spots, and strangely, for the first time, she began to hear the music. Really hear it. The beat seemed to grab at her, hook her, spin her, turn her around. It caught her legs, her heels. Toe, toe, around, around. Toe. Toe. Suddenly, she felt herself smiling. Swinging. Why not! Why the hell not! Her hair swung around, whipping her neck as she turned again. Hips. Hips. Wash that man! Wash that man!

Go, Jennifer, go. Her face was set in a cool, satanic smile. Cool, Jennifer, cool. Toe, toe, touch, touch, swing . . . And there was no one there but her connected to the girls next to her. All connected, a string of silk spun off from the piano and the trumpet, wild, whining, part of it, part of each other. Jennifer flashed a smile to Denise, and she smiled back, her short hair shaking as she danced.

Finally the music whined its last beats, and the girls, one girl, turned and arched their fingertips at the lights. One beat. And the music stopped.

It was over. Jennifer and the others stepped back out of

the lights. Crazy, Jennifer had not made the final cut, but she was bursting with a kinetic joy that had happened somewhere on that third page of sheet music. Of course, she was glad she had come. How would she have known otherwise? Suddenly she had to say it. She turned to Denise, "That is a good dance!" Silly words, simple, but didn't they tell Denise that Jennifer loved swinging! Feeling her hair whip around her neck. Sensing the line dancing together.

She nearly forgot David, who was facing the six girls sitting on the dais. "You've worked hard for two weeks," he was saying to them, "I wish I could say you would all make it, but the stage is small. Please, try out again next year. A lot of you did real fine."

Then, the six picked out were not the dancers!

Jennifer felt the bewildered look on her face.

"The rest of you," David was saying to Jennifer's line, "you began to look like you might work together. I've taken two more than I had thought, but you had that certain look. We've only started, mind you. It will be a lot of hard work yet. Be here tomorrow at four. That's when we begin."

Jennifer knew something had begun already.

"JUST TRY a spoonful."

"Janet, I really don't want to."

"It's only soybean sprouts and lettuce, Jenny."

"And honey."

"All right. So, it's soybean sprouts, lettuce and honey. It won't hurt you."

"Look, Jan, you're you. You like Haydn and Picasso and bean sprouts with honey. I'm me, I like Hammerstein and Wyeth and hotdogs and mustard . . ."

"Try it."

"Do I have to?"

"You have to."

"All right."

(pause)

"Well?"

"I don't like it . . ."

"Oh, Jenny."

"But, I don't *not* like it either."

"Well, that's a start, Jenny. That's a start."

OUTSIDE, THE WIND was blowing winter chills through fall ripened orange and red ripened leaves, tumbling them end over end across the walk and into the narrow street. As she walked out of the hall and onto the stoop, Jenny could see her breath; it was that cold already. She hunched up into her down jacket and rubbed her hands.

"I say football," she said determinedly, looking back at Chris buttoning his jacket with a football tucked under his arm.

"Come on, Jen, let's go for a walk," Chris coaxed. "Look at the wild geese. Ducks? Blue jays?"

Jenny closed her eyes and shook her head. "If I'm going to play Saturday against the seniors, I'm going to be good."

Chris danced down the stairs in front of her, hitting the football into his opposite hand. "I couldn't interest you in a game of post office?"

"I'm serious, Chris," Jenny said, frowning as well as she could in the face of his patter.

"In that case . . ." Chris zipped up his jacket ". . . let's get down to business." He slapped her heartily on the back. "Let's see how you receive." He ran down the walk, ahead of her, faking passes. "Ready, Cooper?"

Jenny puzzled for a moment.

"Over there, Cooper, over there." Chris nodded across the lawn. "It'll come like a bullet!"

Jennifer started running at a diagonal in the direction of his nod, running as fast as she could. Chris stopped, faded back, then threw the ball in an arc over her. She could see it spinning above her, then ahead of her. She reached with her legs, gathering up swatches of leaves and ground in leggy sweeps. Then, in a last push, she jumped for the spinning ball . . . and touched it as it spun off her fingertips.

"Damn!" she muttered, running after the end-over-end ball into the neighbor's driveway. "Damn!"

"Not good, Cooper, not good." Chris tucked his hands into his plaid wool jacket and ran over to her. "But you touched it; that's something!"

He met her frown.

"Now, this time — " he put his arm around her shoulders, the whispering coach " — pull it in from your fingertips. Tip it in." He rolled the ball across his large hand, catching it from his fingertips. "Like so."

Then he pushed back from her, faking passes into the air. "All right, Cooper. Go."

Jenny started out again, racing, cutting across the walks into the next yard. Again when it began to drop she leaped and touched it, but again it spun off, tumbling away from her, and tumbling her into the leaves.

Chris laughed. "Closer, Cooper, much closer."

Jenny just lay there, her face tucked into a pile of leaves.

Sweeping the ball up with his hand, Chris ran over and squatted next to her. "A walk, maybe?" he said.

Jenny turned over, picked the leaves off her shirt, one at a time, deliberately, and stared at him. Just stared. Stubborn.

"Again," she said. She got up and walked almost martially across the lawn.

Chris shook his head and sighed. "All right. All right, Cooper." He stood up with the ball tucked under his arm, spit on his hands and shouted a singsongy "Let's go!"

Jenny ran again, checking over her shoulder as the ball spiraled out, lower this time, but faster. She checked and ran and checked and, as she and the ball narrowed toward each other, she checked and reached and had it! But suddenly it was as if the ball had energy of its own; it seemed to seize her, and as she hung on, it tumbled her into a roll that ended against a stump. Still, she held tight.

Jennifer smiled smugly as she sat up cross-legged, the ball cradled in her arms. "Yeh!" she said, grinning at Chris when he ran over.

"I can see it all now in the city newspapers — Sunday edition. Two-part headline. Powder-Puff Star — A Receiving Genius!" He was squinting and nodding into some far-off future, which right now approximated the Hoffmans' front yard across the street.

Jenny got up, wiping her jeans with one hand, clutching the ball with the other.

"Or" — Chris went on — "Second Stringer Wins First String Spot in Opening Game. Cooper All the Way!" He was an on-the-spot newscaster. Jennifer just smiled, shaking out her jacket and flexing her shoulders as she started to walk.

"Or" — and he trotted up behind her and whispered — "Girl Halfback Looses Ball to Tricky End." And he gave her arm a good nudge with his shoulder, freeing the ball which tumbled to the ground. Then he darted in front of her, snatched it up, and started running down the sidewalk.

"Chris!" Jenny started to run after him.

"Part of the game, Jenny!" he called as he threw his arm out straight to deflect her hands.

Jennifer dodged around to his other side and grabbed at the ball, nearly knocking it free, but Chris spun, his shoulders hunched around the ball, and suddenly swerved into a field. He was in full flight now, his long legs sweeping over the brittle brown weeds, dodging from right to left, gathering speed, stretching out ahead of her. Jennifer kept running and running, but Chris ran faster and faster and farther and farther.

At the edge of a woods, he leaned back against an oak tree and raised the football in one hand. "Touchdown!" he shouted, looking back at Jennifer still whipping through the high weeds, still running. When she caught up she stopped full against him, out of breath, puffing. He smiled down on her and put his arms around her.

"Now, you want to go for a walk?"

Jennifer still panted, harder, trying to catch her breath.

"Now . . ." she said, looking up at him ". . . I want to try that play again."

"WE'VE SEEN THE MOVIE. We've read the play. Can you all agree Macbeth is evil? From the minute he listens to the old hags, he sets out to kill King Duncan and take over the Scottish throne. The man is EVIL!"

"Oh, I don't think so."

"What? Is that you, Jennifer, speak up, speak up, so June sleeping in the last row can hear you."

(laughter)

"I just think the thought that he might be king was something that crossed his mind. A lot of people have so-called evil thoughts cross their minds."

"Ah-ha . . . you, Jennifer Cooper, have had evil thoughts?"

(laughter)

"Sorry, sorry. All right, go on, Jenny. We're listening."

"I think Lady Macbeth eggs him into the murder; she is really the ambitious one."

"The evil one?"

"I hate those words, Mr. Peterson. Evil. Good. I think Lady Macbeth is the more ambitious in the beginning, and I think Macbeth tries to fight it, but gets caught up in it."

"So in the end they are both ambitious!"

"Not exactly. Macbeth's murders begin to multiply and drown the country. Killing sort of creates its own mess. Lady Macbeth senses it first."

"Proof! Jennifer, I need proof!"

"I think she starts to change when she learns the nobleman Banquo is gone. Wait. I'll find it."

"Proof! Jennifer Cooper, proof! Sorry, fans, I've seen too much Shakespearean acting this week. Got it, Jennifer?"

"Yes, here it is. 'Naught's had, all's spent where our desire is got without content.' Lady Macbeth was willing to stop with the murder of Duncan, but Macbeth isn't. He doesn't trust anyone. Anyone."

"Yes?"

"So he goes on killing anyone in his way."

"And Lady Macbeth?"

"She can't stop him, but her guilt gets the best of her. They almost switch positions. In the beginning Macbeth has the big conscience; he sees daggers that aren't there. At the end Lady Macbeth is the one seeing things. She can't wash out the red spot on her hands — blood guilt."

"And so who is evil?"

"Mr. Peterson, I don't think that's the point of the play!"

"Quite so, Miss Cooper, quite so."

Part Four

ONE HUNDRED AND TWENTY MILES left until Charlottesville and still waiting. Still not asleep. Still feeling the train running through the night. Three hours more, but it could stretch to four. I wonder what he's doing? Sleeping? Taking a shower? Waiting, too? I wonder. Four hours is a long time when you've waited so long. But then, so is five minutes.

Seat 21 and 22 are passing the time together. Seat 22, gray hair and sneakers, has taken her brown paper bag and plumped herself next to the soldier. An unlikely pair, she hiking up her rummage-sale double-knit socks every other nod, he brushing his fingers through his too short hair, whispering and eating ham and pickle sandwiches together. Passing the time.

Maybe strangers are a relief. Maybe I should have said, come on over, Seat 23, tell me all about your kids, your ulcers, your tennis game. A stranger, yes. It all adds up either way, and sometimes looking at someone you care about can be too much like looking at a mirror. You start to look at a grandma or a mother or a Chris to see who you are. Hey, am I good? Am I funny? Am I smart? Mirror, mirror on the wall, tell me, am I here at all?

If the answer is yes, Seat 23, you're flying. You're the greatest one of all. But what if the mirror is misty? What if it's cracked? What if you can't hold so many mirrors in your hand? Or what if they don't seem to be there at all? Do you disappear?

Like I said, mirror, mirror on the wall, tell me, am I here at all?

THE HOUSE WAS EMPTY, except for him. Jenny had known that when she had said she would come. But empty had never felt like this before. The overstuffed maroon chair where Mr. Cochran always sat was still pressed into the form of his fat body. The cat, its torn ear flicking nervously, stretched in the middle of the floor, unafraid of feet. The clock tocked noisily, at different rates it seemed, so hollow was the responding silence.

"Well, where's the refrigerator?" Jenny said with a lightness she hardly felt. "If I'm the cook for the night, show me my tools." It was a laugh really. She had barely cooked, even at home, but when Chris had said his parents were going to be out of town for a week, she had promised him she would help him out. Nothing seemed wrong with that. After all, they had been friends for two years now. It wouldn't have even been necessary to tell her mother she was going to a piano lesson, but parents needed some foolish assurances.

Chris didn't answer her. When he took her coat, he ran his hands down her bare arms and turned her toward him.

"The refrigerator," Jenny whispered, pushing him away playfully. It had always been hard for her to have him close. Always. It was a feeling she had, a feeling somewhere between pain and excruciating joy. But it scared her. Her defense was words, or laughing, or playing.

"I'm not hungry, Jenny." He pulled her back against him. Jenny could feel him warm, touching her. She closed her eyes to think or feel, one of those things, then looked up and grinned at him.

"I am. Ravenously."

"A four-syllable one for the occasion!" He had not moved.

Jenny wasn't used to seeing him like this. He was almost someone else. But not quite. She sensed him, and she started to back away teasingly to the kitchen, when he drew her arm out and pulled her gently, patiently, to the floor.

"I want to say hello."

She had no words.

And he kissed her as gently as a breath on her neck and on the bottom of her chin, and she felt her hands go around him, and he laid her back on the floor and brushed her cheeks with his mouth, and her ears, he brushed. And his hands moved around her waist, gently and evenly, and she had no words. They were at the edge of her mind. She tried to reach them but they skimmed off, slow motion, tipping but falling around her in splinters of touch. And she fell and fell in an airy silence.

For a moment she opened her eyes and looked at him, this human being she knew so well and didn't know, and he said, "Now?"

And something from inside her that she didn't recognize said, "No, please, no," and she felt tears running warmly down her cheeks because she hated the voice. The tears burned at the corners of her mouth as she felt his hands inside her sweater, touching her skin and pulling her down into that cavernous warmth, but the awful voice said it again, "No," it said, "no," and she didn't know why it had come back again. Or from where. She didn't know the tones or the cacophony of that voice, and she hated it, and even as the tears streamed down her cheeks she pressed his hands to her bare breasts.

And he looked at her, not understanding, wondering, too, whether she were her hands or her voice, but as he pulled himself gently across her body and she felt the wonderful weight and the smell of soap, the voice grew clear and tearless.

"I'm going home," it said. And Jennifer began to recognize it, even as she hated it.

THE VENETIAN BLIND CLAPPED lightly as the open window behind it let in a gentle, moist wind, the sound of someone's lawn mower already cutting its swaths up and back, smells of coffee perking and far-away kitchen voices, explaining voices. But Jennifer pushed it all away, trying to hang on to a dream. Something of a fair, wasn't it. She tried to sink into the remnant of the feeling. Wasn't she running from booth to booth at the fair? Shooting dented, pocked-shot ducks that dappled by in an unending line. Trying to knock over a lavender dog higher than she, and failing, then hitting it between its shaggy eyes. Running and running, grabbing yard-long hot dogs from a white hat, a perspiring white hat. Putting a head-sized quarter into a mechanical fortune-teller where a steam shovel dipped into a treasure of rings and grabbed a red diamond one for her. Running over the beaten-down grass and the puddles left from yesterday's rain into a stark white building that said HORSES LIVE HERE, and finding them inside, running on a track with peculiar little carts behind them. Running alongside of them, the dust cuffing up, blowing in her face as she tried to pass the chestnut with the green cart. It was important to pass it. It was . . . but suddenly there was a noise out of cadence, a soft shuffling of slippered feet.

Jennifer opened her eyes slowly, annoyed, but she didn't move. She watched the short, thick figure bending over, scuffling about something. Jennifer shook her head from side to side, more annoyed. She didn't belong here in this bed, watching the scuffling figure. She belonged back there at the fair, and she was growing angrier. Why didn't the scuffling go away before the smells of popcorn and hot dogs and sweat and dust faded? But then she realized. They were gone. That fast. Gone. Only the feeling was left, the feeling, but even that was draining out of her, being replaced by the scuffling of the bent-over figure.

"Grandma!" Jennifer said, rather sharply.

The figure turned, a smile spread across her pudgy cheeks. "It's about time, Jenny," she laughed. "It's ten o'clock. My, you got in late last night." She turned back toward the windows and opened the slanted blinds, then went on picking at something, her back to Jenny.

"I have nothing to get up for, really," Jenny was trying to even out her tone. But it was difficult.

"Just a beautiful day. Another sunny day. I'm going to pick roses before I go shopping today; the yellow Cumberlands are in full bloom." Her Grandma Stokes went on chattering even as she busied herself with whatever it was she was doing.

Jennifer stretched up on her elbows to see what it was. And then couldn't believe her eyes. Grandma was going through Jennifer's suitcase. Through her clothes.

"What are you doing?" She couldn't control her tone.

"I'm just getting your dirty clothes, Jennifer. You've been here two weeks and haven't washed a thing. I'm putting an extra load in anyway and . . ."

Jennifer threw back the covers, went over to the suitcase, and shut the lid. "Please, don't!"

But Grandma laughed. "Jennifer, Jennifer, still my little mussy one." And she opened the lid and went on picking out Jennifer's underpants and bras and shirts and . . .

"I said, don't . . . I really would rather sleep now and do my own clothes later." She had never spoken like this to her grandmother before, but there it was. Had she any right coming into the bedroom when Jennifer was asleep? Had she any right going through her suitcase? She pulled the suitcase toward her and looked back into her grandmother's face.

The tight little roll of thin brown hair that encircled her head was pushed up into a net, and her pudgy cheeks seemed drawn as her mouth closed in a line. She said nothing. She just looked at Jennifer.

Jennifer took the suitcase and pushed the pile of dirty clothes back into it, not in any particular fashion; she just jammed them. Then she slammed the case shut and fastened the clasp.

Her grandmother watched her, not moving.

Jennifer took the suitcase and pushed it under the bed. Then she threw back the sheets and climbed in, pulling them around her shoulders, and closed her eyes. Was there even a remnant of the fair left? She scoured her mind for a thread, a touch, a taste. But she kept feeling her grandmother leaning against the end of the bed. She wasn't going away. She wasn't moving at all.

Jennifer waited. The clock tocked noisily on the dresser. But her grandmother didn't move.

Suddenly Jennifer pushed the sheet back with her feet.

"What is it, Grandma? I said I will do my clothes. I will do them. Please, let me alone!"

But her grandmother said nothing, just started to stand up slowly. Heavy to being fat from eating whatever was left on the plates of all her family — the leftover potatoes, the pork chop fat, the gravy — she stood up, a round, bent ball, pushed her apron down, and took a deep breath. She avoided Jennifer's face.

"Grandma?" Jennifer asked. She looked into a face drawn not into an angry look, but an agelessly, infinitely sad look. Jennifer had never seen such a look on her grandma, her strong grandma, her sturdy grandma. And for the first time Jennifer noticed her grandmother couldn't be over five feet tall. She was tiny.

"Grandma," Jennifer asked again, frightened now by something she couldn't put words to. She climbed out of bed and put her hands on her grandmother's soft, round shoulders. "I just *like* to do my own clothes, Grandma," she said in a mollifying voice. "I'm used to doing them."

"I know, Jenny," she said, without anger or rancor, without wanting to change anything, without any tone at all. "I know, honey."

And Jennifer tried to stop her and wanted to go back five minutes to have a chance to say it all again, to have another chance to say to her grandmother, "Oh, please do my laundry — my shirts, my socks, my pants — no one washes it like you do, no one hangs it out to dry on the back line so that it will smell fresh, no one folds it like you do, importantly, in my suitcase." But it was too late. And Jennifer knew that it was too late.

THE BARREL REIGNED on a square of bricks between a hedge of rosebushes and a picnic table covered with bowls of chips, its fat paunchy self being emptied by a hefty shadow with a cowboy hat who leaned on the spigot while a cluster of shadows pushed glasses under it in a continuous stream.

But the group sitting in a circle on the lawn, just out of the back lights, had their own pitchers. Jenny hadn't noticed the pitchers or the circle when she sat down next to Gail Ashby. They had been good friends ever since suffering six weeks of David Blake in dancing rehearsals, and parties weren't all that common. A familiar face was a happy sight, particularly since Chris had disappeared with a basketball. But now she could see it was a circle and it was closing. Everyone's legs were crossed and their glasses were set in front of them on the grass as if something were going to begin.

Uneasily, Jenny started to push back, looking over her shoulder for Chris.

"Stay in, Jen," Gail whispered to her. "It's a blast. Really."

"Look, I have no glass, Gail," Jenny whispered back,

inching out. This was no time to admit that she had never had a glass of beer, only once when she was about three. "I'll see you later." She thought she saw Chris over by the garage with a group of shadows playing basketball by the garage light.

"No, you don't," a voice boomed. It was Tommy Hyland, standing in front of her, a giant shadow with a raised glass in his hand. "This game is for the fearless, the hairless . . . the brave. (laughter) "Give her a glass." (more laughter)

The cowboy hat at the barrel threw her a glass which rolled into her leg. There didn't seem to be any way out.

"You'll love this game, Jenny," Gail whispered, planting her glass firmly in the grass in front of her. Tommy filled it, then went on to Jenny's.

Jenny watched her glass being filled, watched the dark liquid rise to the top, watched the foam dribble over the sides. It seemed no part of her, but clearly it was. She felt a kind of fear, mixed with a heady excitement. Maybe it was because she didn't know what was going to happen.

Tommy paced the inside of the circle.

"The game goes like this," he said. Clap, clap, click, click, a chorus of hands started behind him. "We each have a number." Clap, clap, click, click. "One, two, three," he chanted, tapping the head of each person in the circle. "When you click your fingers, call your own number (clap, clap, click, click) and someone else's. That number answers and calls a new number." Clap, clap, click, click. "It's called Concentration." His eyes seemed to bulge in the shadows as he tapped Jennifer number four and went on.

She looked a last time for Chris.

"If you fail" — Tommy was still talking — "the joy is yours, a cup of the finest brew this backyard barrel has to offer . . . to be filled up again with more of the finest brew, etc." Clap, clap, click, click. He turned. "By the way, the game tends to get faster . . ." He smiled wickedly and sat.

Chris came up as he did. Relieved, Jenny caught his pant leg. "Hey," she whispered, "we'd better get going, Chris."

He looked around the circle, a little embarrassed. "Not me, sweetie, Concentration is my game. Why, in the summertime, I am MR. Concentration." He smiled at Gail. "No one can trap the old M.C." He squatted down at the end of the numbers, across from Jenny. "Number fourteen, on deck."

Then there was no way out. Jenny suddenly felt so trapped. She looked around the circle of shadows; she couldn't even see any faces.

Clap, clap. "One-three."

It had started.

Clap, clap. "Three-five."

Clap, clap. "Five-twelve."

It was already growing faster.

Clap, clap. "Twelve . . . ah . . . six."

"Chug!" the circle cheered, one voice. A tall girl Jenny didn't recognize laughed and poured a glass of beer down her throat. Then the circle fell quiet again and the clapping started.

Clap, clap. "One-ten."

Clap, clap. "Ten-*one*."

Clap, clap. "One-*ten*."

(laughter)

Clap, clap. "Ten-three."

Clap, clap. "Three ... um ... five." Gail, caught.

"Chug!" the voices shouted, louder, still one voice. Gail tipped her mug, part of her beer spilled over her chin and jeans, her eyes squinted shut. Jennifer wondered if sometimes a number were never called. Maybe number four wouldn't be called. Suddenly she didn't want it to be called. Not four!

Clap, clap. "One-three." The clapping drove the numbers faster and faster. Clap, clap, "three-seven," clap, clap, "seven-four." *Four!* Jenny!

Clap, clap. "Four ... four ..." Jenny couldn't think. Not of a single number. Nothing.

"Chug!" she heard the voices demand. "Chug!!" Gail's, the cowboy hat's, Tommy's, Chris', separate but one voice. And she sat there.

"Hey, Jenny, chug!" It was Chris.

Jenny looked at him for a second, not sure why; then she grabbed up the mug and poured it into her mouth, but the bitterness was beyond what she expected. She coughed out the first swallow in a spray.

"CHUG!" the group demanded again, louder, not satisfied.

Jenny took the glass again between two hands, took a breath and poured it down her throat. She felt it running down her cheeks, felt it wet on her hand. She smelled the beery smell strong in her nostrils, but she chugged until the glass was empty. She had hardly put the glass down when it was refilled and the group had already begun again.

Clap, clap. "One-five." Clap, clap. "Five-one."

Gail whispered to her. "Great, Jen. You were great."

Jenny nodded, licking her lips. Relieved, excited, angry. All of those things.

Clap, clap, click, click.

Chris whispered across. "Great beer drinker, Jen. Great."

Jenny nodded, clapping in time.

Clap. Clap. "Ten-nine."

Clap. Clap.

"MISS COOPER, look what you've done. You've taken off the pink number-four copies and put them on the number-three hook."

"I was told to put the pink copy on the number-three hook, Miss Lorenz."

"Wrong, Miss Cooper. The yellow copy goes on the number-three hook. That goes to the bookkeeping department. The pink copy is filed."

"That's not what I was told yesterday, Miss Lorenz."

"Well, I'm telling you — now, Miss Cooper!"

(pause)

"This is a very busy dry cleaning shop, Miss Cooper,

perhaps you'd rather work somewhere else after school. A place where such things don't matter!"

"I'm sorry, I'll put the yellow copy on the third hook, Miss Lorenz."

"We'll see, Miss Cooper, we'll see."

T HE BLUE CHEVY backed out of the driveway, screeched its turn, then honked down the street, hands waving out the window. Jennifer waved back from the front stoop. It had been a lovely night, a crazy night — three guys, two girls, none of them dating, just laughing and laughing for three hours, two hamburgers and two shakes each. Over inane jokes: why did the elephant wear sneakers while swinging tree to tree? Answer: he didn't want to wake up the neighbors.

Jennifer just stood smiling. She really had been able to forget. She took out her key. Funny, somehow she hated to go in: that would end it. Smiling a last time at the spot where the car had screeched away, Jennifer turned the key, glancing down the street as she did. The brown pickup was parked in a driveway five or six houses down, away from the street light.

Jennifer couldn't believe it. She looked at her watch

under the porch light. It was already twelve and the house was dark, but, quietly, she pulled the key out, ran down the stairs and over to the shrubbery of the houses to avoid the street light. Then she ran over to the truck. The door was pushed open for her.

"Chris!"

He reached over for her hand, and pulled her into the pickup.

"What are you doing here, Chris? You're not supposed to be seeing me." Jenny sat back against the door, a broken six-pack between her and Chris. The three-hour talk they had had a week ago still stung her. ("My father thinks I should date around," he had said. "My father wants me home more," he had said. "My father . . .")

Chris nodded, lightly. "Yes, but I miss you now. That's all."

He tore a can out of the pack and handed it to her. She shook her head. She wanted to touch him, let the back of her fingers stroke his face. Instead, not sure why he had come, she folded her fingers in her lap. "Didn't you go out tonight?"

He sat back and sprawled his legs under the steering wheel. "Yeh, I did. Nice girl. It was fine." He was staring out of the windshield; it had started to sprinkle lightly. "But . . . it's like I said, I miss you now."

It was strange really, how words mattered, how they pushed and pulled, how they moved. Jennifer sat back, watching the drops of rain gather into beads, then heavy with their own weight, wind down the windshield. She could feel him watching her. There were old patterns they each knew. Sitting back stopped them, but the no-words created a hollowness that made the raindrops on the roof sound tinny and loud.

Jennifer leaned forward and looked at her watch. "I really have to go, Chris," she said, reaching for the handle. "My parents . . ."

Chris took a long drink, then wiped his mouth with his wrist. "Look, what I wanted to tell you about was . . . I went to a jazz concert last night. Stevie Karo's group."

Jenny turned. "That's great, Chris." She looked at him for a minute, long and long. Then reached again for the handle.

"And . . . ah . . . after the concert . . . I stayed on." He turned to look at her, his knee folded across the seat. Seeing her wait, he went on. "I met the group backstage, just went there, all alone. Karo was just leaving. And while I was shaking the guy's hand, I just happened to mention that I played drums."

Jenny watched him. "Leave it to you." Suddenly she knew the words he wanted. Maybe that was why he had come. "Yeah. Then he said, 'Are you doing anything tonight? Like now?' Karo said that!"

"You're really crazy, Chris." Jennifer felt like his mirror.

"I know. I know." He grinned. "And so we went to his motel room. Tiny. Just four walls. Full of smoke. It was full of smoke." He was in his stride now, full of words. "And all the fellows in the band were there — a trombone, clarinet, trumpet. Some women, of course. Smoking."

Jenny nodded. It was as if he were blowing up a red balloon. And if the reflection he saw in her were real enough to him, excited enough, he would let the balloon fly.

"Well, all of a sudden this clarinet player over in the

corner starts wailing, his back to everybody, see. Then, the trombonist picks up and starts playing counter wails to him. Sweet, Jenny. It was sweet . . ."

"It sounds sweet, Chris."

"Then, I ask if I can play the drums. The guy says, yes. Just like that. I take the sticks with these twenty- and thirty-year-old guys, and I play a tat-atat-atat-tat that fits in like . . . like fingers pulled across a harp. Sweet, Jenny, sweet."

Jenny nodded, knowing that sweetness, pleased for him. Showing it.

"So, Karo himself comes over. Can you believe it. He comes over with his trumpet and suddenly there we are, bouncing sounds off each other. Him all over his keys. Me all over the drums. It was the most sound, Jenny. The sweetest. The best."

He was staring up at the roof, savoring it. The most . . . the sweetest . . . the best. It seemed to soothe him, murmur to him like the whispered patter of the rain on the car's roof. Jennifer let him alone with it, but then he looked at her. She shook her head. "What can I say? It's fantastic, Chris, really!"

He settled back again, satisfied. "Yeh," he repeated. "Fantastic."

Jennifer looked at her watch in the glove compartment light. It was 12:30, but now it was she who felt the pull of old patterns. She was waiting for something. Other words. Then he touched her arm.

"See, they can't keep us away from each other."

Jennifer grinned, letting him take her hand. Those were the words.

J ENNY PUSHED THE CHAIR back from the dining room table, deliberately, noisily. Her mother looked up from the pool of peas she was trying to coax over toward her potatoes, but she didn't say anything. Jenny's father angrily turned the next page of the sports section.

But Jenny refused to allow the new adjustment to silence to last. Not this time. There were things to be said, and she was going to say them. She was not going to be put off by her mother's tears. She was not going to be put off by her father's angry edicts! She was not . . .

"I'm going," she burst out. Like that, the last phrase, a determined promise to herself.

"You are not going," her father looked up and said through clenched teeth. She could see it made him angry to have to say it.

"It is the last basketball game of the year. Everyone will be there . . ."

Her father closed his newspaper and left the room.

She was not going to be put off; she was not going to be put off. Rising, she followed him into the living room, her pulse beating in her throat.

"Dad, I really will go, whether you want me to or not."

Her mother was behind her, trying to hold on to her arm, but Jennifer slipped out of her grasp and her father spun around.

"Look, you can go to as many basketball games as you like when I can be convinced you are not going with Chris Cochran. I've had enough of him. Do you hear?" Her father, usually a quiet man of few words, spewed them out as if they had been stored for a year . . . more. "Whatever he says to do, you do. 'Sure, I'll write your papers for you, Chris. I'll pay your way to the dance . . .' "

Jennifer stared at him, not blinking. "He is busy sometimes and broke . . ."

Her father laughed. "Who says? Him? God, Jennifer. Maybe that's the worst part of it, you believe anything he says! He says he's played with Stevie Karo or Doc Henbush or Shorty Hawn, you believe him. He's selected for some mysterious state swim team, you believe him. He can't see you until midnight, you believe him. If he told you he was flying to Jupiter in a Greyhound bus, you'd believe him. Can't you see what he is? He's a con man, Jennifer. A con man."

The wrongness of what he was saying stung Jennifer. She closed her eyes and started, slowly, measuring the words. "I don't do whatever he wants me to do . . . I don't believe just anything . . . I only do and think what I want to . . ."

". . . and that is what he says!"

The wrongness, the wrongness.

"You're like some puppet or some ventriloquist dummy! Jennifer, why . . . don't . . . you . . . see . . . him . . . for . . . what . . . he . . . is?"

Jennifer stared at him, her cheeks flaming. "I would go to the game anyway tonight, even if Chris weren't going to be there. It's the last game of the year. There are parties afterward. I am going. Why shouldn't I go? Why shouldn't I?"

"Why? Because you're losing yourself! And I won't have it!" His dark eyes flashed angrily at her and his voice was loud and frightening, but Jenny didn't move.

"And what will I do at home? Play the piano? Watch television? Look in the mirror at myself? What? What?" Jenny felt her chin reach out as she threw her questions at him. "And who are you to decide what I am? Even if I were a parrot, a puppet, or a dummy. It is my life. Mine!"

Her father flinched at the "mine" as if it were thrown at him. He took her arm, pinching it with restraint. "No. Not yet, it isn't. Not yet. It's my life, too. And I don't like what I see. Chris Cochran expects you to believe him. He expects you to be there waiting for him. Any place. Any time. He expects you, Jennifer! . . ." And his voice fell, suddenly. "Don't ever be expected, Jenny, because you are part of me, and it turns my . . . stomach!"

Jenny felt his angry words lash her, but they only made her more sure of what she had to say. She was not going to put it off. She was not going to put it off.

"No! You're wrong, Dad. You're not part of me. I am only me. And I love Chris!" Why did those words come out so uncomfortably. She reached the banister and said them again louder. "I love him. And I want to be with him, no matter how it makes you feel. No matter!"

And her lips felt stronger as she said it, and it was not her father's dark look that made her turn and run up the

stairs. It was not. It was having to have said it out loud, to
have put words to it. All that feeling, trapped and narrowed and compressed by stupid words. She hated it. And
she hated him.

"HELLO, JENNY?"
   "Yes, Chris."
   "Sorry I couldn't get to you yesterday, but . . . I've got
incredible news!"
   "Yes . . . what is it?"
   "You remember that team I play baseball with on Sun-
days across town?"
   "Sure, I do."
   "Well, a guy from the New York Yankees farm team, a
Jerry Hamilton, was there, scouting."
   "Oh . . ."
   "Really, honey, really."
   "But . . . that's wonderful . . . when did he see you
play?"
   "Last Sunday, yeh, it was last Sunday."
   "But last Sunday we went to that picnic in Northville
Park."

"Well . . . two Sundays ago then. Anyway . . . when he called yesterday and said it was Jerry Montgomery speaking, I didn't know who he was."

"Montgomery? I thought his name was Hamilton."

"Hamilton . . . Montgomery. Anyway . . ."

"Yes . . ."

"Well . . . he wants to see me this Sunday, wants to see me work out at first base . . . with the team, of course."

"Of course."

"It's only for the Yankee farm team, but, I mean, let's be practical, I'm not going to make the big league right off."

"Probably not."

"But then Seth Walters did. Remember him? He went right into the major league. Was he a character! Do you remember how he used to dance around the field and throw those signs at the umpires? Wow, he was the greatest character. I'd be like that."

"Yes." (the greatest, the best, the most . . .)

"I can just see it, Jenny, I'd take that first base like no one else. I'd whistle and dance between pitches. I guess the crowds would love that, eh, Jenny? Can't you see it? The little girls in the first bleacher row with signs: 'Chris Cochran you adorable clown!' That would be it: the adorable clown. Pictures in the Sunday sports section. I'd hardly be able to move through the crowd on a double-header. Can't you see it, Jen?"

". . . so when are you going to see Mr. Montgomery?"

"Who?"

"The talent scout."

"Oh, yeh, well, I'm supposed to see him on Sunday . . . I'll call you after I do."

"Yes, Chris, call me after you do."

9 : 4 5. FEET SHUFFLING, lockers slamming, test at 10. William the Conqueror, 1066, Battle of Hastings. Chris. Chris. 1066, Harold, the defender, William the Conqueror. 4:00 dance committee. Chris. Pick up cleaning. Chris. Test at 10. 1215, Magna Carta. Chris. King John. Maybe an A, no, maybe a B. Feet shuffling, lockers slamming, oh, Chris.

LEGS AND ARMS and skirts and books and heads and music pounding and a steering wheel and flying cigarettes somehow finding the right mouth and fingers tapping. The car felt as if it had been packed with all these things, not carefully, but thrown in, helter-skelter, and once thrown, they had picked up their own rhythm which beat out or flew out as the thing moved. A beat. A beat.

Jennifer tried to discover it, squinting into the smoke.

"Jennifer, you're a crazy lady coming here with us!" Sue yelled over the music, flicking her cigarette ash onto a preciously empty spot in the corner of the car. "Lady, we are crazy!"

A beat. A beat.

"Crazy nice," Jennifer shouted back and smiled. Sue and she had been friends a long time.

Sue picked up a bottle of wine and guzzled it as if it were a Coke. Karin in the front seat grabbed it away from her and stared at Jennifer.

"Did you guess there is something we wanted to tell you?"

Karin looked like a mask to Jennifer with her blue-lidded eyes and bluish lipstick, and Jennifer found herself moving her head to one side as if that would help her see past the mask.

"No," Jennifer said. Maybe she had wondered why all of a sudden she was included in one of their Friday nights. Always friends, Jennifer had spun off socially somewhere around the seventh grade when her chest stayed flat and Sue's and everyone else's seemed to blossom like spring buds.

Jennifer felt her hands tighten in her lap.

"We don't have to tell her right away," Sue snapped angrily at Karin.

Another head turned around, its long hair swinging as it turned, "I say, tell her now," the head said, lazily, somewhat bored, "I don't see what the big deal is anyway. So someone says she's being screwed, big deal."

There was a sudden silence that broke the beat, that stopped the bottle, that immobilized the hands and heads and legs and cigarettes.

Jennifer found herself biting the inside of her cheek, looking at Sue.

"Oh, boy, Ann, you are cool," Sue was saying. "Really cool. You remind me of my Uncle Horace sitting on my mother's vanity chair. Very cool."

The head shrugged.

Sue looked at Jennifer, straight, no plaster of Paris on those cheeks or across those eyes.

"It's just, Jenny . . ." Jenny was remembering the time Sue and she poured a bottle of perfume in the bathwater when they were twelve. "It's just that you think so much of Chris Cochran, and you have for two years, right?" Then once she and Sue dared each other to strip and jump in the lake in January. "And you think he's a super student and a super athlete, and a super friend. And he may be a lot of those things." Once Sue and she had drunk a gallon of warm lemon juice to stop a cold and had gotten sick instead.

The mask suddenly flicked a butt out the cracked window. "Look, don't make this a melodrama, Sue. Get on with it. I want to get somewhere. Anywhere!"

"It's just that Chris Cochran is telling the whole locker room that he's laying you every weekend. I know, I can see your face, you don't want to believe it. But, I've heard it from four different guys, Jenny. It's true."

"Well," Jenny heard herself saying. (It must have been her voice; the words were coming from her mouth. She could feel them.) "Sue, I really thank you." She suddenly began to worry that her legs and arms were interfering with the beat. The beat. "I would want you to tell me. I didn't know. I . . ." Her rhythm was so bad. Not even syncopated. It marched across the legs and arms and cigarettes. "And I needed to know." Maybe Haydn would have been better. Maybe Hammerstein. No, they all fit and didn't fit. Jennifer sat, suddenly limp, feeling the limpness, the sinew string out and sag in its amorphous, beatless way. Jennifer sat.

"WHO DO YOU THINK you are?"
"Jennifer Lynn Cooper."

"Look, I don't need your smart answers. I am the teacher here. Do you understand that? When I say we will have a paper due on Friday, we will have a paper due on Friday. Is that clear?"

"That's clear. I just felt, Mr. Neilson, that with the math and history quarterlies the same day, it was a lot . . . and . . ."

"Well, maybe that's your problem. You think too much. A little less thinking would serve you very well, is that clear?"

"Yes."

"Yes Mr. Neilson."

". . . yes, Mr. Neilson."

Who do you think you are? Jennifer Lynn Cooper. Jennifer Lynn Cooper. Jennifer Lynn.

Part Five

STRANGE. The train steward just asked me how old I was, and I looked right at him and said, "Sixteen." I have no idea why. I haven't been sixteen for nearly a year. Perhaps I'll wait until he comes back on his four-car route and stop him. "Wait a minute," I'll say. "I made a slight error. I am seventeen years old. Seventeen and teetering, but seventeen."

Teetering. A funny word. But then Charlottesville is only sixty-three miles away. It really is the countdown. No more broken postal hooks. No more station stops. Straight through. No-nonsense. The train has even picked up speed. The trees seem as if they are spinning away from the railroad car: the ones up the hill, stodgy, barely moving, these by the tracks, dancing away.

I like that word anyway. Dancing. Good for people, not just trees. Better than teetering. The one is deliberate, isn't it. Yes, dancing is deliberate. Dance, people, dance. Flip out, shake your hair, your head, your breasts, your feet. Or more. Be a clown. Dance on your toes with your painted cheeks and the red triangles under your eyes that show you've been crying.

That's only right. The dance and the tears go together.

No, it's even more than that. The tears are part of the dance. And you can sit like those trees on the hill and let the train be the mover and wailing cries will leave you behind. Or you can dance, sweep, even with the tears streaming down your painted cheeks.

❈❐❈❐❈❐❈❐❈❐❈❐❈❐❈❐❈❐❈

C HRIS!"
    "Oh, hey, Jen. Ah, what are you doing here in the parking lot. (Hey, guys, hold on, I'll be there in a minute.)"
    "I thought maybe you'd come out this way."
    "Oh, yeh?"
    "Yeh."
    "Well . . . I did!"
    (pause)
    "What's up?"
    "A lot of people have been talking to me lately."
    "Oh, yeh. Well, don't believe everything you hear."
    "That's how I feel about it . . . you see some of it's about you and me and. . . ."
    "That sounds like a dull plot."
    (pause)

"You see, Chris, I really want to believe you. I trust you."

"You should. I'm trustworthy. (OK, OK, I'll be there in a minute.)"

"I guess it has to do with what you think we mean to each other. What we are to each other . . . I certainly am having trouble with words tonight."

"Hey, Jen. That's heavy. Don't try to box everything. Nice and light, Jen. That's cool. Keep it nice and light."

"Sure, Chris. But I really want to talk about . . ."

"Look, Jen. Joey's driving. Let's talk another time. I'll call you. OK, Babe?"

IT DIDN'T LOOK like a gymnasium, and it certainly didn't feel like one. Tonight it was Oz. A yellow brick road wound itself around the room, and a cockeyed Dorothy-like house sprang up behind the band like a comic hotel. The band blared, the mixer blending some wailing sounds.

Jennifer walked ahead of Charlie, her green crepe dress swishing quietly as she walked. She purposely held her head up. Pinky, her ninth-grade camp counselor, had taught her that. "So, if the world kicks you in the teeth, hold your head up; remember it's not what the world thinks that's important. It's what you think."

It's what you think that's important. It's what you think that's important. It's what you think. It's what you. Jenny felt the strobe light dancing its colors over her face and arms. No one was dancing yet. That took time. And it was dark, she could barely see who was there. Time for that, too.

"Hey, Jenny!" Donna called to her. She smiled at Charlie.

Keep your head up. Keep your head up.

"Would you like some punch, my little chickadee," Charlie whispered in her ear. Jennifer smiled at him and nodded, head up. He winked at her. Jenny smiled more broadly. He really was a marvelous thing to look at, probably over two hundred pounds, his triple chin jiggling happily with each joke he threw to his ready audience, his toes pointed out, rocking him comically from side to side as he walked toward the punch table.

Everyone loved Charlie Simmons, whether he was cracking his hundredth joke in his W. C. Fields accent or strumming his banjo at the canteen. In a way Jenny loved him, too.

"Hi, Jen, where's Chris . . ." Mary Jane started, then seeing Charlie come up behind her, she shook her head. "Sorry, never mind. Hi, Charles, you old dog!" she said and trailed off behind her date.

The head must remain high at all times, quoth the Lord. No, it couldn't be the Lord who said that, only Pinky after lights out.

Jennifer sipped at the punch. "You did a great job with the decorations!" Ben Savant called out as he danced Donna by. "Are you the wicked witch or Dorothy?"

"That's for me to know," Jennifer laughed back.

You see, even laughter is possible, if you keep your head up.

"Shall we dance, Dorothy my dear, the cowardly lion said?"

"Oh, yes, dear Lion," Jennifer purred. It was rather like that, too. It would have been so much more difficult with anyone else. How could anyone not dance and enjoy and laugh with this roly-poly lion. Dear lion. Dear self. Because it isn't easy, dear lion; some pains hurt beyond hurting, beyond breathing.

Jennifer caught her breath, refusing to take that path. Blocking out those words. And for the moment she let her head be empty. She stepped away from and toward Charlie as the electric guitars strung out a rolling whine of music. Occasionally she smiled, across at Beth — she had helped paint the road, at Rocky Devito — if he hadn't helped her put the frames into the cockeyed house, they'd still be lying in the gym basement. A nudge to Janet — Janet's first date. That was great.

But then Charlie caught himself in the lights and something about the music and lights and people gathering on the floor sent him off. "Hey, Dorothy. Look at this." Charlie inched toward her, skipping on one foot, gingerly, then spinning, all two hundred pounds.

"All right, Charlie," someone yelled. "Fly!"

The guitar picked up the excitement and pulled the strings in a webbed crescendo that sent Charlie in sweeping turns around Jennifer; then he caught her arm, spun her the other way, and did another skip and spin.

The crowd loved it. "Charles. Charles," they hooted. "Go!"

It was like pumping blood into him. He went.

Jennifer went, too, smiling, wondering about the sudden circle she found herself in. Almost enjoying it. Almost forgetting. She didn't even see the clot of kids newly arrived at the door. Not right away. But the next time Charlie spun her around, winking as he did, she turned and saw Him. Chris. He was smiling at Alice, perfect Alice, smiling at her in his three-piece suit. And as Jennifer tried to keep dancing, she suddenly knew what he smelled like, all showered and soaped, and it hurt her knowing that.

"Hey, Dorothy!" Charlie chanted.

She tried to smile, to keep on dancing. Some part of her tried, but some terrible hurt was swelling in her, and even the edge of her eyes caught him holding Alice's arm, laughing with her, not knowing Jenny was there. Even though she was in the middle of the dance floor, not knowing.

Perhaps if he knew, he would care. He would be sorry he hadn't asked her. She would know if she could just catch a glance. Just a glance. Suddenly she had to dance so that she could see his face, and the next time Charlie swept her around, she spun even farther out.

Until she was two feet from the two of them, him in his gray three-piece suit, and Alice in a quiet blue silk gown, stately and walking importantly with her head up and laughing, gently. Jenny nearly came to a full stop just to catch his eye. To be sure.

But his eyes were gray. There was no anger in them. She was not even a form he recognized. The mirror he looked into was his own. He didn't even notice her. It was worse than anger. It was being invisible.

"Dorothy, hey, check this," Charlie said, turning her away from them. Jennifer shook her head gently at him. Hey, lion, this can't be Oz. It hurts too much.

THE AUDITORIUM WAS vaguely like a zoo at feeding time. The same sweaty smells, lightly varied since they were brewed by gym classes that didn't save time for showering and heavy doses of perfume administered at the change of periods. Noises. Hooting of friends across the room. Ripples of secret laughter.

Jenny slumped into the chair, her knees up against the seat in front of her. Lois was chattering at her in the next seat, Donna behind her, pouring trivia into her ear. Jenny was thinking about the announcements. Maybe it was foolish to care whether you made the Honor Society or not. Maybe it was. Probably it was. But Jenny's guts announced their own standard. They cared, every fiber of her: her liver, her pancreas, her stomach, even her feet, cared whether she made it or not.

She had worked hard. High grades . . . or high enough. Homework, done. Extra work, done. Activities for the school, done. Everything, done. Completed. And she not even seventeen yet. It mattered to her pancreas, so what use was it discussing her brain's decision?

"I just don't think I have a chance, Jenny. I don't have any extracurricular activities," Donna was saying.

"But all A's are hard to beat."

"But you have mostly A's and B's and activities, and you were a prom chairman. What is there against you?"

Jenny shrugged. To herself, to her mirror, to her journal she had stated flatly, "How could you *not* make it!" Still, there had to be looks. Appearances. "You never know," Jenny said, but she didn't believe it. She had to make it, that was all. She had done all of the right things, and she had done them well. She had to make it.

Lois slunk into a position, imitating Jenny. "I just wonder who could have it in for *me*."

Jenny looked at her, puzzled. "What do you mean?"

"That's all it takes, Jenny. One faculty member black-balling you, and you're done."

"But how could a faculty member make that kind of judgment? How could a faculty member know enough about a student?" Suddenly Jenny could hear herself caring.

"They don't have to. One spitball at the wrong time. They don't have to justify themselves, Jenny, they just have to vote."

A shadow was nipping at Jenny's mind. "That's ridiculous, Lois. Teachers have to have some balance; they are not going to make a judgment that could affect a student so seriously. They are just not. I mean, there are teachers I haven't gotten along with, but I would trust them not to make that kind of decision. God, Lois, you are ridiculous."

NATIONAL HONOR SOCIETY

Gail Ashby
James Corrigan
Stanley Ferret
Donna Henry
Lois Jorgensen
Ann Marie Maron
Henry Orthway
Alice Richards
Janet Smith
Jeffrey Spenser

IT WAS JUNE HOT, thick with it. There was only the slightest murmur in the trees; the leaves, too, were heavy with it. Jenny laid the black gown across the back of the seat and pulled her light cotton skirt up over her knees. Even the bath powder she had dusted herself with after her shower wasn't helping. Already she felt sticky.

She flipped off her sandals. If a cop stopped her, she'd flip them on again.

She edged the shift into "neutral," started the car, then shifted into "drive" and started down the street. Her mother thought it was silly to try to get this in before the graduation services at seven, but Jenny didn't. Her Grandfather Cooper couldn't get to her graduation. She'd get part of it to him.

"It won't even matter to him," her mother had said. "He doesn't know anyone anymore, Jennifer. You're just rushing yourself when you don't have to." "I have to," Jennifer had told her. There was no point in arguing about it. Jennifer knew from her insides that she had to be there. Arguments usually needed reasons. She had no reasons. None you could list and win points with. She just had to be there.

Jennifer put her elbow out the window. It was all so green. The lawns with their manicured bushes. Even the patches between the sidewalks and the street. The wind blew her hair back. After Jennifer had so carefully blown it dry. That was funny. It was being reblown for certain.

Jennifer turned down the wide avenue, busy with its yellow buses advertising Lark cigarettes. Already past six o'clock, the stores were all closed. How often she had driven this street, how often. And walked it before that. To the one-room library at the corner of Lyons and Maple with its sweet smell of dried glue and its creaking floor. To the drugstore with its rows of comic books. The light turned, and she eased into "drive" again. Even the buses looked familiar. Probably she had ridden every one, to and from school. To the stables to ride Danny. To the park to meet Chris. Or other friends.

A rebuilt Volkswagen nosed itself in front of Jennifer and she hung back to make sure its snubbed tail made it. She didn't feel like fighting for space today. It was 6:10; she had until 7:30 to get back to the school. Just enough time.

At Altar she turned into the rutted, dirt road. It was an anachronism, this street among all the paved, neat, housed streets. It was as if someone in some governmental office had seen all the cottage shacks on the street and decided that people living in such houses shouldn't need pavement on their street, sidewalks across their mud.

In front of 354 Jennifer pulled up and slipped on her shoes. For a minute she just looked at the little white cottage, painted freshly, long-necked petunias straining to stay upright in the flower box that hung on the side of the porch. The swing on the porch was empty.

She reached for her gown and easing herself out of the car, put the gown on. Underneath, she felt the heat trapped in beads forming on her skin. It was June hot. She tucked the strands of hair behind her ears and started across the uneven walk.

"Grandma!" she whispered through the screen door. She could smell that familiar smell of fat, stuffed chairs that had borne the burden of cigar smoke too long. Today it was mingled with the heavy fragrance of peonies, arranged in a huge painted vase on the coffee table. "Grandma!"

A tiny, bent form came into the gray room, wiping her hands on her apron. "Jenny? That you?" Grandma Cooper had decided she really could not leave Grandpa, even though she had wanted to come to graduation. He just couldn't be left alone.

"Oh, honey, you shouldn't have come," she started and pushed the screen door open for Jenny to squeeze in.

Jenny didn't want her to say that. It gave her the same feeling as when her mother had said it. That it was no use. And Jenny wouldn't accept that. She wouldn't.

"Oh, you look lovely, Jenny. Your hair so soft and pretty. And look at that gown. Didn't Grandpa always say you was the smartest girl?"

Jenny felt some awful tears in her. It was terrible to hear him spoken of that way. He wasn't gone. There were still things to be done. He was still there.

"Won't you sit down, Jen. I'll get you some iced tea. That will make you feel real nice." Grandma Cooper liked to feed Jennifer. It usually took the place of words they had never found. But Jenny hadn't come for iced tea.

"I want to see him, Grandma."

"Oh, Jenny, he's not feeling too good today."

"Please, Grandma."

"Well, sure, honey, if you want to." Her grayed hair was not quite all caught up in the bun at the back of her head. Locks fell out around her ears. When she led Jenny into the bedroom, she seemed more bent than Jenny had remembered. Her back arched up almost as high as her tiny head. She looked tired.

At the door she pushed aside a faded blue curtain and held it for Jenny.

"Jack, Jack, Jenny's come. It's her graduation day." How peculiarly she had said it. As if she were talking to a child. It made Jenny angry to hear.

She inched around Grandma quickly to say her own hello. But she didn't say anything for a second. Of course, it was he, but it was too hard to believe all at once. When she had come over to see him two weeks ago, he had just come home from the hospital and was too tired to see her. And she had no idea. No idea.

It was as if he were shrunken, lying there on his fresh pillow. All the bones of his face seemed to take the prominence away from the flesh that once laughed and blew smoke rings into the air. And his hands stretched in a bony angularity next to his side.

Jenny closed her eyes for a minute. It was Grandpa. It was Grandpa. It was "Grandpa!" she said for herself.

His eyes looked up at her abstractly, but Jennifer was so pleased to have reached him that she went on. "Have you heard from Arthur?" she said with a smile. He didn't smile back. His eyes had wandered over to her grandmother.

"Water" he said to her, not demanding but evenly.

She turned to reach a pitcher set on the top of the dresser.

"It's my graduation day today, Grandpa. I made it. See, I'm wearing a black gown." Jennifer smiled and looked self-satisfied, but he had closed his eyes.

Jennifer sat down on the side of the bed. She was bigger than he was. She looked at the clean sheets pulled up around his neck. A breeze blew in the open window, billowing in the curtain. The tiny clock ticked at the side of the bed. Ticked loudly. She stared at his face. His thin lips looked so dry, but when his eyes had closed, Grandma had just stood with the glass of water. Waiting.

Jennifer realized that this empty space of time was June heavy, too.

"Grandpa," she tried again.

His eyes opened. Grandma went over to him and lifted his head up for him to sip the water. Then she fluffed up the pillow and eased him up onto it. He allowed it all to happen with disinterest.

"Grandpa, I got an A and four B's this last marking period. Great way to end high school. Right?" she said lightly.

Suddenly, his eyes shifted and he looked at her as if he had just had a brilliant recognition. "I know," he said. "You're Letty, aren't you."

For a moment Jennifer just looked at him, feeling tears pinch at the edges of her eyes. Then she sat back and stroked his thin hand, his dear hand. She nodded to him, yes, and as if relieved, he put his head back on the pillow and closed his eyes again. It was all right. She was glad she had come. It was for someone else she had come. He would have so appreciated it. It was for him.

J ENNIFER WALKED through the night-wet grass, toeing the tufts slowly. Well, then, it was over. The speeches, the hugging of old friends, ten-year old friends, teachers you liked and didn't like, pretended affection for

Uncle Ed, the dean. The clinging to the last minutes of being together, hands in hands, arms around waists, shoulders touching. It wasn't that it had all been so wonderful; it was just so hard to leave before you touched the next base.

A hazy moon hung boldly in a black sky dusted by the milky way and more. The house's eyes looked shut. Shut tight. Asleep. Somehow she even felt as if the house were no longer a part of her, something she had left behind. The green shutters hanging at a tilt. The too-large spruce covering the front windows. The upstairs Cape window. Her window. What had been her window.

Then Jennifer caught sight of two figures sitting on the steps, just shadows, but she recognized them.

"Mom, Dad?" she whispered, careful of the next-door neighbors, still inches away. Her mother was sitting a few steps down from her father, her head leaning against his knee. A cigarette glowed and dimmed. "What are you doing up?" It had to be two o'clock, maybe later. They had left the graduation ceremony as soon as it was over, before Jenny had gone on to her parties.

"Oh, just talking," her mother said.

Jennifer wondered what two people who had been talking for twenty years still had left to talk about, but she sat down a step up from her mother, not saying anything more. Just listening. The three of them. Crickets noisily chirped against a blank velvet silence. There wasn't even any wind. Just crickets, endlessly, but marvelously familiar right then, like the street light down the block casting its familiar shadows across the narrow street. The same shadows of cars parked in front of the same houses.

The Chevrolet sedan. The Dodge wagon. The fire hydrant sprawling grotesquely, familiarly, across the street.

The three of them there, familiarly.

"What did you think of the ceremony, Dad," Jennifer finally asked. Her father and she did best with direct questions from each other.

"All right," he said simply. His cigarette glowed red as he drew in on it.

There was a waiting pause.

"It made us wonder what you are going to do, Jennifer," her mother said carefully. *Us.*

Jennifer resettled herself on the step; the question pushed somehow. "Oh, I don't know," she said evenly. "I have so many things I would like to do . . . I might . . ."

"You should go to college." It was her father's voice, low, almost sulky. "Just like I should have gone."

Jennifer drew in the night air, feeling that old tightness. Feeling the quick responses on the edge of her tongue. The anger. *Should.* But she went on.

"I've thought about business school and laboratory technician school. And of course, I like dancing . . ."

"That's worth nothing when you add it up," the shadow said quickly. "Nothing. A college degree, now that is worth something."

Jennifer turned around, ready, quite prepared to lash into whatever word battle he cared to launch. Ready. But then quite unexpectedly she saw him there in the shadows. His mouth tense, not really wanting to parry but wanting things for her and him and not knowing how to get them. His small shoulders bent close to her mother's head, the two of them, maybe only one, wanting. But not knowing how.

Jennifer felt like a part of them, and a part from them. And she felt her shoulders sag and the anger flow out of her, away from her. And she went up to him, sitting on the step, his cigarette stuck securely in his mouth, the tough little guy, and she put her arms around his shoulders.

It was not so hard to do. "You may be right, Daddy," she said in a low soft voice that was becoming more familiar to her. "And I will probably make some pretty horrible mistakes, big ones, but I have to make them. I have to figure it out for myself." She looked at him through the darkness. "I just have to." And she stood up and kissed him on the top of his head. "Good night, you two," she said, and she went into the house, leaving the shadows leaning together in the night.

"Name?"
"Jennifer Cooper."
"Age?"
"Seventeen."
"Previous employment?"

"After school at a dry cleaners and . . . ah . . . baby-sitting."

"I need someone who can manage this office for the entire month of June, maybe longer. That means, keep these bills in order, type correspondence, but when I'm not here, it means handling anyone that comes in off the street."

"You think you can handle it?"

"I think so."

"You *think* so?"

"I'm sure I can, Mr. Corey."

"I've seen a lot of wishy-washy teenagers, frankly. The kind that follow their whims. No sense of responsibility. No sense of other people. No sense — period!"

(silence)

"Are you one of those?"

"I don't think so, Mr. Corey."

"You don't *think* so."

"I'm not, Mr. Corey!"

"There! That's what I'm looking for, a girl with gump-tion. Someone who knows what she wants. Knows it! KNOWS IT!"

Part Six

P EOPLE ALWAYS DO THAT, don't they? Crowd
the aisles before the train even comes into the station,
before the rhythm ends. Seat 22 is already vacant, just
potato chip crumbs to prove anyone was ever there at all.
Seat 23, too; Beige Suit is standing, showing the attendant a string of pictures, the three kids I missed seeing.
Even Sneakers is at the water cooler trying to stuff her
paper bag into the cup disposal.

Then it's time, isn't it? There are no more miles. I seem
to be left not with the red balloon, not even the willow
tree, only the questions.

It's strange. For days I waited for the telephone to ring,
but when it didn't ring, and it didn't ring, I finally stopped
waiting. But I never waited for a letter, and it came.
Postmarked "Charlottesville." "Dear Jenny, I guess you
didn't expect to hear from me. (I had stopped waiting.) It
is strange to come to a place where you don't know anyone. (There is a time to stop waiting.) Edgar Allan Poe
went here to college, but was kicked out. I hope I do
better. (Words.) What I really want to say is I feel sorry
about so many things. About the phone calls I didn't
make. The prom. Not saying good-bye at graduation.

(Words.) I think I always missed you. It's more than having to do my own English papers. I miss you walking next to me. I miss talking to you. I miss touching you. (Funny how words can matter.) Come to Charlottesville to see me, April 28? There's a dance. But we don't have to go. Please, Jenny. I need you. Love, Chris." Love. Words.

Some said that they used to be such a good team, Cooper and Cochran. What does that mean? That they danced well together? That when he led, she followed. When they soft-shoed into the spotlight, the crowd cheered. (Question: When is a crowd like a mirror?) Or does it mean more than that? Does it mean she tended not to fall on her face when he was there to hold her up? Does it mean that he didn't fail his English papers when she was there to write them? That they walked like a London Bridge, supporting each other. They were once friends. That's the bottom line. Does that mean they were friends, or they are friends, or they will always be friends?

Or is it irrelevant?

No matter. It all adds up. The date must be kept. Hell, Jennifer Lynn, what is the green of you? Maybe it is time to stop looking in mirrors.

The serpentine wall wended its way lyrically along the walk. Shadowed trees rustled behind it, catching the wind in their leafy nets. Jennifer walked next to him. Him. To think it, to say it somehow made her skin cold. Him. She didn't have to look at him in his gray jeans and unbuttoned shirt to know him. His face already tanned from afternoons playing ball. His hair tipped blond from the spring sun. His uneven white teeth, quick to break into a hopelessly easy grin. His feet bare, comfortable on the damp formal walk.

She knew him. Even now when she had not seen him for nine months, she knew him. She knew his pulse, his need to win, the bronze of his skin, the smell of him. She knew him.

"It seems strange to have you here."

How uneasy his words seemed, he who knew all the quick words.

"It seems strange to be here," she said.

He knew this wall, the crush of the trees in the wind, the dark-eyed buildings crouched over the weekend, waiting for the burst of Monday morning and classes. It seemed strange that there was something they didn't know together. That was what was strange.

"I was really happy you decided to come." .

A date to be kept.

"Yes."

"On football weekends, this place was a crowded mess, cars piled on cars . . ." he went on, searching.

"The streets are narrow," Jennifer tried to help.

"Yes, the streets, and people partying all over the place. They have great parties. Pot by the jar and the booze runs out the doors."

"Sounds hard on the doors." Jennifer grinned.

"Everyone invites people down for those weekends. I usually came alone and played the drums for the Sigma Rho band. I might join that house. I like those guys."

(pause)

What were the words for this person she knew and did not know?

"You'd really like one of those weekends."

Jennifer suddenly smiled up at him. "I bet I would. Do they play rock or jazz or . . ." Pleased that she had found some words.

"Rock, mostly. It's a blast, really! A blast!"

(pause)

A funny thought of her sitting in Janet Smith's living room with the Brahms on at a whisper wouldn't be pushed aside. Rock or jazz was what she had asked him.

"I've been playing a lot of classical lately, two-piano stuff. With Janet Smith, since both of us are home."

"Oh, yeh?"

(pause)

"Of course that's when I'm not counting bills at the advertising agency!"

"I bet you like having the money."

"I like the empty space, the time to think, I guess."

She felt suddenly hopeful, as if maybe they were warming up. Maybe he would understand how her head was filled with choices. And ideas. And colors. Too hard to pick a college when you didn't know whether to be a lab technician or a dancer. When you didn't know whether you liked biology or English literature. Suddenly she looked directly at him, hoping for words. She even started them.

"I think it takes time for a person to get herself together. Sometimes I just think about possibilities. I don't even read some nights. I just think. Do you?"

That grin. "Not when I can avoid it!" He laughed. Then, seeing her mock frown, he caught himself. "Of course, I still like to argue philosophers . . . Kant or Descartes, the old is-the-pine-tree-that-falls-in-the-forest-heard argument!"

"Is it?" Jennifer asked, still smiling.

Chris looked at her. It felt like a parry. It was.

"Well, I personally think in subjective realms."

"Subjective?"

"Well, that a person perceives . . . oh, Jenny, stop. Stop." For a moment he just looked at her, then pleaded, "Come over here." And he touched her. In the lamp light shadows that stretched across the curving walls, he touched her arm, bringing her against the cool night brick. Then he lifted her face and looked at it, all of it, and slowly kissed her skin. Her eyes, the side of her nose, her cheek. And he kissed her lips, warm and wet. And she remembered. And it was like sinking into each other, yin and yang, curled enigmatically around each other with all their strange and different pulls.

He kissed her.

"I love you so," he said in her ear. "That is what I wanted to tell you."

She felt her fingers around his neck, felt his soft blond hair in her hands. "I know. I know." And she felt the knowing.

"It was awful. Sometimes I would be in the middle of an exam and I couldn't think. What did it matter what the pH level of putrefying milk was? What did any of it matter? I couldn't write anyone. I didn't try out for any sports. I felt horribly incomplete, like something hadn't been done." He touched her face, running his finger under her chin and down her neck.

"I know that feeling," she said.

"It's like the world will simply go on, erasing the traces, if you don't hold it for that something you have to do."

She laid her head on his shoulders. He used to say she fit there in the angle of his arm. But now was different from "used to." He was using words, real words. And she allowed the thought to cross her mind, the thought that with this person, this sweet soap-smelling person, this crazy unpredictable person, she felt whole. Finally. It was an incredible thought.

So she didn't move, hoping to trap the thought in this moment, to have it always. Him.

But another couple walked by, barefoot, in blue jeans and open-necked shirts, their deliberate informality also defying the vined formality of the walk. The girl with hair long and flying was explaining something to the boy, her hands describing vast sweeps into the air, the boy laughing, his hands in his pockets, his head nodding; he knew, he knew.

And Jennifer smiled at them even though they had stolen her moment and substituted theirs. Jennifer and Chris leaned apart and started to walk again through the gateway into a dark, narrow walk that seemed to cut between private, heavy-lidded houses. He held her arm, relaxed, nothing tentative in his touch. Not now. He had heard some sort of answer from her.

"This university really is a peculiar place, Jen. A mixture."

"Certainly, it is a lovely place." Jennifer slipped off her shoes.

"Lovely. Yes, I guess that is a good old-fashioned word for it. Some of our southern gentlemen still talk about the

Civil War as if their fathers fought in it: 'At Chicka-mauga, Old Burt fought ten hours straight, etc., etc.' Then you find out Old Burt was his great-granduncle three times removed."

Trivia, but somehow important just now. Jenny just listened.

"One roommate, Dave, is crazy. He has girl friends in every college east of the Mississippi; he's gone every weekend."

"Oh?"

"Comes back just in time for his tests or exams. And aces every one. Crazy."

Jennifer suddenly realized a strange thing. Chris was talking with the slightest drawl.

"I've got no time for his stories, that's for sure."

There it was again. Time, "ta-om." Sure, "shu-ah." It nipped at her mind as she felt the cooling pavement on the bottom of her feet, felt its comfortable roughness under her toes.

"You know I'm working out for the swim team."

She looked up at him. Baseball was his game, but he had been a strong swimmer.

"I know it's hard to believe, but *they* came after me." He grinned, embarrassingly, at her.

"I don't even know how they heard about me, but the coach called me one night, about two months ago, and said he needed someone to swim the free style."

Jennifer felt her arm drop away from his arm, felt her arms begin to swing evenly in the night air.

"The first time I ever swam for him, he pulled me aside and said I'd swim first string in the fall. At least the fifty-meter crawl, but maybe the medley, too. Great coach. He really *made* this winter for me."

His words had a jauntiness about them, a swing.

"Sometimes after practice just he and I would go down to the pub for a beer or two. You know, put two swimmers together and you have a good night out! Not bad for a freshman, huh?"

Jenny stretched her fingers as she felt the blood warm in the fingertips, and she breathed deeply of the honey-suckle blossoms that drooped heavily on their leafy arms. She could even smell the mint behind them, springlike, tiny and fragile in the earth, already mattering. Not to be overwhelmed.

"Am I boring you with all this, Jenny?"

"No, go on." This was part of the date she had to keep. She had not always known it, but in the fragrant night she knew it. And she thought for a moment that she might have to tell him how suddenly green she felt. She might have to tell him how his words fell over her, spattered on her shoulders, fell unimportantly around her ankles, as she walked toward the end of the University lane.

CHARLOTTESVILLE — RAILROAD OFFICIALS TODAY ANNOUNCED THAT DUE TO RISING COSTS, BEGINNING JANUARY 1, SERVICE ON THE JAMES WHITCOMB RILEY WILL BE CURTAILED. LOCAL RAILROAD OFFICIALS UNOFFICIALLY ADMIT THE CHANGES WILL PROBABLY RESULT IN DISRUPTION OF SCHEDULING BETWEEN THE TWO CITIES.

THE RAILROAD PRESIDENT, WHO COULD NOT BE REACHED, RELEASED A STATEMENT WHICH SAID THAT . . .

Y

Gauch
Green of me

Date Due